Client Affairs

G EORGE M C COY

PAGE PUBLISHING, INC.
New York, NY

First originally published by Page Publishing, Inc. 2018

ISBN 978-1-64350-177-2 (Paperback)
ISBN 978-1-64350-178-9 (Digital)

Printed in the United States of America

In memory of my grandfather,
Warren Eugene Gourley,
for helping spark the fire of my imagination,
teaching me what little I know about women,
and loving me unconditionally.

CONTENTS

PROLOGUE

Fifteen years of marriage, and this is how it ends. Her identity smashed into smithereens in seconds. She was a wife, a mother and . . . an empty shell of who she used to be.

She had raised three children with him, but only one of them was his. Just eleven, thirteen, and sixteen, but all looked at him as a father. Surprised? No. But . . . it was a shallow experience. For months, Jerry felt the distance grow between her and her husband. No, they hadn't had proper sex in years now that she thought about it. But there was no dramatic walk in on him with another woman. There was no word from one of her friends that they had seen him necking some woman at a coffee shop. No, even in fucking up their marriage he was lame. Excitement was never part of Donald's personality even when they were dating. A simple blood test to reveal the reason for an itch that was read to her by a Mormon doctor that looked at broken vaginas every day of his adult life was how she found out.

Perhaps he would deny that he gave her chlamydia. Of course. He would say that she had been fucking around or that she got it from a toilet seat. She knew better though. Driving at a pace brisker than was advisable on the old windy country road, she pondered what she was going to do. Her eyes drifted away from the road she should be looking at to gaze toward cottonwood trees lining a fence enclosing several horses. She could simply leave. Pack up the children, run to Portland to see her mother, and be done with it. She could even put it under the veil of going to see her mother for the weekend and not let him know it was over until she was there. She could change the locks and simply not let him in. She could tell him to leave and see if he actually would. She could kill him . . . No. She couldn't kill him. She wanted to with every fiber of her being, except that she couldn't do that to her daughters. She could pay him back. She thought of the neighbor across the street who often stared at her for far too long. He was older, maybe fifteen years older than her, with a shaved head and a black goatee. The neighbor had, in reality, been nothing but creepy to her . . . even if somewhat attractive for an older man. More exciting was the idea of seeing Donald's face as he walked in on her and the neighbor embrace, moments before climax. To see the hurt in his eyes that she felt now.

Jerry had always felt that she had been an attractive woman. At thirty-five, she hardly felt old. She had long blond hair, dyed from her natural brown several years ago at Donald's request. She always wore makeup, at Donald's request as well, to highlight her large brown eyes and even did everything to keep herself at the same weight she had been when they got married, if not lower. She had always tried to be at her best for him even when they were not doing well. It was part of her self-image.

Her black Ford Focus pulled slowly into her driveway. Donald's truck was nowhere to be seen. He wasn't due home for several hours. A security guard at the local college, he worked late every night. At least he *reported* he was working. He certainly kept himself busy in one fashion or another.

They had built the home together. They raised the money for a down payment and purchased the land plot as part of a local development project. Several areas of the home were of sub-par workmanship as they had elected to try to finish several areas of the home themselves. Those were the happiest times of their life together. Throwing paint at each other. Making love within the empty house in between putting up sheet rock. But now the house simply reminded her of Donald's cheapness. The paint on the ranch-style house was beginning to peel. The gutters were full of various debris, but luckily, it did not rain in Klamath Falls very often. The lawn had been neglected for several months. Donald has a garden in the back he watered every night, but he was too lazy to do much else.

She walked through her driveway toward her door. Absentmindedly, she stumbled with her keys in her hand, staring off into the distance to the right of her house at an elderly woman who was watering a small vegetable garden just outside of the gate to Jerry's backyard. Jerry entered the house and sat on the tan couch in the living room. She turned on the television, mostly for noise, and let the issues of the day stew in her mind, clicking through some of her favorite channels more due to routine than to actually find something.

She decided that the best thing she could do is reduce her feelings to writing. None of the kids were at home—the two eldest at cheerleading practice and the other daughter at soccer practice, taken by her grandparents. She grabbed a small pad off the refrigerator door and began to write.

Donald,

I got blood test results from my gynecologist today. I think you already know what they said. I am going to take the girls with me to my mother's for the weekend so I can think about things. I am not interested in working this out, but I know that you are a special part of all the girl's lives. I think that it may be best that when I get back you are gone and we can work on figuring out a schedule for the girls between our houses.

Jerry

She crumbled the letter and walked it over to the recycling. She tossed it in shaking her head. No. Donald had never been violent per se, but he had frightened her. She thought better about alerting him to her intentions. She would think it through before she made her decision.

She drew a bath. Bubbles, wine, candles, the whole works. The bath water was burning hot to the touch. She stepped in anyways.

Slowly the bubbles faded one by one, and the wine bottle grew emptier and emptier.

She was floating in ecstasy. An ebony-skinned man was embracing her, moving his hands up and down her body with his muscular arms, strangling her in pleasure. She felt his lips touch her breasts as his hands caressed her inner thighs. His lips moved from her nipples, to her neck, to her lips. She felt his teeth playfully bite her lower lip. His right hand moved behind her hair as he grabbed a handful of her blond locks. She moaned with pleasure as his manhood entered her.

She awoke with a gasp, choking on soapy water. She looked through the open bathroom door and caught a glimpse of the alarm clock in her bedroom—nine thirty. Jerry quickly got up and grabbed a robe. There was a dead silence to the house. As she pulled the white cotton robe over her body, she walked down the hallway to see a faint light coming from the kitchen.

"Hi, dear," Donald said, dry and slow. The slow drawl of his voice made her pause.

Donald was a short man with a slender frame. He was chubbier than he had ever been at any point during their marriage, but he had been one hundred pounds when soaking wet most of his life, so it wasn't saying much. His short stature coupled with his beginning of a gut made him look oddly proportioned. He had deep-sea-blue eyes and sandy, natural, blond hair.

"Where are the kids?" She gave Donald a piercing look. They had passed the point of social niceties in their relationship years ago. The words "I love you" were reserved for three occasions: their anniversary, any time either of their sets of parents was in the room, and when they passed toilet paper to each other when one had forgotten to refill the roller.

"At my parents. I sent them over there tonight. I figured we could use a night together by ourselves."

Donald's tone was again dry and calculated. "Is that okay?" Donald inquired. A weird smile was on his face. It was oddly forced.

"Well, ya, I guess so." Jerry wasn't really sure what was going on. Donald did know she had been to the gynecologist today. Perhaps he already knew that she had found out. "Um, let's watch a movie?"

It was a question, not a statement. She didn't want anything to do with him at all, but his tone had frightened her. It wasn't that he was ever truly scary. He didn't yell much, and when he was truly angry, he would mostly drive off in his truck for a few hours. No, it was the calmness that made her weary. He was always jumpy, and rarely had he wanted anything to do with her when he got home from work. She felt it was best to play along until she could get the girls back in her care and then take off.

"How was work?" She wanted to make small talk to try to keep him unaware that anything was wrong. Before he had been home, she felt a fierce fire build in her. Now she was afraid. She had never felt more uncomfortable in her life.

"A girl got raped in a stairwell on campus today. I was the first responder. Actually, it was kind of a mess. Ton of paperwork," Donald said again in his monotone voice.

Jerry thought about his tone. How could he talk about it like that without emotion? Then again, she thought about the effect that it might have on her. The morose nature of the day would have been incredibly draining, and perhaps all her emotion would be drained as well.

"I'm sorry to hear that. Is she okay?" Jerry asked with genuine concern.

"Not really." Donald shrugged his shoulders. "But it was a long day. One of the reasons I just wanted it to be us tonight."

That made sense at least. After a day of that nature, Jerry would want a quiet night too. She felt some of her anxiety subside. Some of it was still lingering, but Donald's abnormal day explained his behavior better than anything else.

"Okay, I'll go pick out a movie. Do you want to get the popcorn?" She had tried to manage a smile but could not. Regardless of his day, she had no intention of making up with him. She still felt that she could not just outright tell him and wanted to just make it through the night to get the girls.

"That's fine. Kettle corn or buttered?" Donald asked.

"Buttered."

Jerry sat on the couch as Donald popped popcorn in the kitchen. She rifled through the on-demand list and found a romantic comedy she believed that they could both agree upon. Romantic enough for a couple, funny enough to be entertaining, but not steamy enough to lead to sex.

The movie was full of lame clichés that Jerry had completely lost faith in. Love at first sight, spontaneous romance, a minor betrayal, and an inevitable steamy makeup scene. Love at first sight led to a miserable marriage fifteen years later because no one took the time to find out if they were compatible. Wanting to fuck someone was hardly a reason to marry them. Spontaneous romance? In real life, sex usually occurred after a shower, and if the sheets were clean, a towel was put down. Even if she just looked at the first time a couple had sex, it was full of awkward moments and giving directions. Oh, you walked in on him talking innocently to your friend who has a crush on him? You poor thing. Try having him give you an infection from banging another woman, you smiling cunt.

As they watched, the only time they touched each other was on accident, both reaching for the popcorn at the same time. When it was over, Donald went to the bathroom without a word, coming back rather quickly. "Let's smoke a cigarette?" Donald offered.

Jerry rose without word and headed toward the back door, just behind Donald. He opened the door to their mudroom and waited for her to walk through first. Jerry walked into the mudroom between the deck and the kitchen, and it wasn't until the light from the kitchen was lost by the closing of the door that Jerry noticed that the back porch light was not on. The switch for both the mudroom and back porch lights was in the kitchen. She stepped toward the nook where the cigarettes and lighter usually sat and stretched her left arm out to grab them as she moved. As she stepped forward, Jerry's left foot stepped on what felt like a crinkled-up piece of paper. She reached down to grab the piece of paper, and her body froze in fear. It was the note she put in the recycling bin earlier that night. As she turned around, a gloved fist collided with her jaw. She felt blood trickle down her face as she collided with the wall.

Jerry collapsed, gasping for air. She began to scream. A size 11 boot hit her square in the nose. She felt blood squirt down her shirt as the impact from the kick had caused her to fall backward, bending at the knees with the bottom half of her legs behind her. With her head on the ground, she felt the impact of the stomp on her forehead only briefly before falling into darkness.

She saw her daughters. They stood in front of her. Their jaws moving without sound as if they were trying to tell her something. As she watched, her mind seemed to suspect that they had been speaking without being heard for a very long time. Like their message was always lost but right in front of her. She had always been so busy with work, so busy with her friends, so busy trying to portray the image of a great wife that she did not truly know her daughters like a mother should.

As she breathed in a large gasp of air, she choked on what tasted like a mixture of vomit and blood. The sudden burst of sound from her lungs hacking up her own fluids had startled the blurred figure standing above her. A flat blunt object collided with her nose over and over again until she descended again into darkness.

Her mother. A plump gentle-faced woman was shaking her head, but from a distance. Then closer and closer, she floated. Her mother's mouth moved. More and more rapidly. She thought, for a second, that perhaps she could hear her.

Gasp! Another mouthful of blood and vomit. She felt her tongue lying in her mouth, barely able to move, but she could not feel her teeth. She sensed that she had been moved and saw little dots of light in front of her. Stars? This time, the attacker did not hit her with a shovel but watched her. Then apparently deciding that she was indeed not dead, he jumped down at her in anger. Her head was cradled in his left hand as his right hand hit her squarely between the eyes.

Her grandmother stood in front of her. She was dead for several years. Jerry was startled as she stood there, not as she was when she passed but as she had been when she was a young child, no older than her girls. She was a beautiful woman with ebony eyes, and hair matched with her ivory skin. She wasn't talking, just looking. She looked just like the black-and-white picture hanging in her hallway, with the exception that her colors shined brightly. For the first time in her dream, she wasn't trying to decipher a soundless message. "What is going on?" Jerry asked, feeling as though one of them should say something.

"You're breathing," her grandmother said.

Jerry didn't understand. "What?"

Her grandmother just nodded and stood in silence.

Jerry stared at her for what seemed like hours before the message began to make sense.

As she awoke, she felt the pooled blood and vomit in her mouth and around her head. She saw nothing with her eyes except streaks of blood and hair. She felt pain beyond measure all over her body. Her left foot felt like it was up against a rough wood surface she recognized as the fence in her backyard as she felt it sway slightly at her touch. She heard Donald working several feet from her. A grunting sound was coming from him. She recognized the sound of dirt being flung through the air and colliding in small piles on the ground. Shoveling. She wasn't sure how long she had held her breath or how long she hadn't been breathing before she awoke. But she did recognize that she had seconds, not minutes, before she would have to try to breathe. She slowly turned her head to the left, hoping against all hope he would not notice. She felt the pool of vomit and blood slowly spill from her mouth. Even better, she felt the blood drip from the hair, covering her noise; and for the first time since she woke, she was able to take a quick breath from her nose. She held her breath again. Not daring to take another breath too quickly, she waited for over thirty seconds. She heard Donald stop digging.

She waited for him to come to her, but he didn't. Instead, she heard him walk back toward the house, or what she thought was the house. Then she was certain as she heard the creek from the stairs. Without knowing what she was doing, she crawled to her knees and attempted to stand and run. She held the scream that should have come from her mouth in with sheer willpower.

She fell to the ground, hard, maybe having moved a foot from where she had been lying. She felt her hand around, which felt as though it had been stomped on several times. She felt her ankles, bloody and . . . cut. Her Achilles on her right foot had been slashed. Even the slightest movement caused her the deepest agony. The left was a mess, but it hadn't been done properly. Moving it caused misery as extraordinary as moving the right one did, but the muscles still appeared to be, at least partially, intact.

She got on her hands and knees. Using all her willpower to stop herself from alerting Donald by screaming, she pushed up on her busted hands and grabbed hold of the fence with her left hand. She got her weight onto her left foot and held her right foot intact with her right hand. She hopped on one leg using the left hand to guide her along the fence. Her eyes were still covered in hair and blood. And in truth, everything would have been blurry without the hair and blood. She was not sure if she would ever see properly again.

She felt a metal handle as she hopped along the fence. Relief spread over her as she realized safety was close, but tension crawled around inside of her as she realized that at any second she could be pulled into what she could only assume was a makeshift grave in her own backyard. She grasped the handle and pushed. The gate swung open.

With all the blood and hair in her eyes, Jerry realized that now her plan was flawed. She had made it to the gate but had little ability to find her way to safety. She hopped straight forward, each hop leaving her with less and less hope. Each hop cost her a tremendous amount of energy as she felt the shock of the landing vibrate through her whole body. The tears in her eyes did nothing to help her vision.

Then her foot landed in a small puddle of water. Her mind raced as her foot sunk into the garden. She was stuck and felt as though her next attempted jump would land her on her face. She began to shake with fear, and faint tears now turned into uncontrollable sobbing. She could no longer hold it in. It was over.

But . . . why was there water here? It was sunny all day.

She quickly fell to her knees and felt around. Her sobbing subsided as she felt a rush of adrenaline and hope. Her fingertips brushed a slimy rubber object. She pushed herself forward, grabbing at the hose. Once in her hand, she pulled it through her hands to assure herself that it was the end of the hose. She pulled along the hose looking for the end. She heard an inaudible but angry voice come from not that far away. Donald. She quickened her pace and found the end of the hose attached to her neighbor's house. She felt a detached nozzle on the ground. She moved her hand up the siding and felt a low window, the kitchen window by her memory, and began hitting the window violently with the nozzle until it shattered.

The kitchen light turned on.

CHAPTER 1

● ● ● ● ● ● ●

Meth Is a Hell of a Drug

"Your honor, this man has been charged with multiple drug-traf-ficking-related felonies, including racketeering. He is a flight risk due to his nationality, and we believe him to have been part of this crime ring for multiple years. The evidence that was presented to the grand jury was overwhelming Your Honor, with returns of true bills on all the charges. Mr. Tornow's argument that Mr. Gutierrez is a family man who was arrested only because he may have been acquaintances of those under investigation for recent murders in the county is ludicrous. We believe that bail should remain at $5,000,000. We would also argue that the court does not have the authority to lower bail below $500,000, as we believe Oregon Revised Statutes 135.242 applies, making crimes that include the trafficking of meth-amphetamines come with a minimum bail amount of $500,000." The woman sat down, red-faced, and looking rather annoyed.

Judge Oswald sat there for a few moments, pondering what the State's prosecutor had said. She looked toward Gary, lowering her black-rimmed glasses, with a piercing stare. "Anything else Mr. Tornow?"

"Quite a bit, Your Honor," Gary replied with a smile. "Ms. Sanders has a misunderstanding of the law. If the court will look at ORS 135.242, section 7, the specific crimes in which minimum bail of $500,000 is required are listed. Mr. Gutierrez has been charged with three counts of racketeering, a crime which does not appear on said list." Gary smiled and turned toward his opponent as he stated this.

Ms. Sanders abruptly stood, dropping several papers to the floor as she did. "That list is not exhaustive. The legislature clearly meant for—"

"Let him finish," Judge Oswald said coolly.

"Thank you, Your Honor. With the minimum bail set aside, I look to Ms. Sanders's claim that there is overwhelming evidence against my client. This is an incredible overreach. If I may be permitted to ask Counsel a question, do you have any physical evidence of these crimes?" Gary already knew the answer.

Before answering, Ms. Sanders looked to Judge Oswald to see if Gary was indeed going to be permitted to ask her a question, an unusual anomaly in any courtroom but Roseanne Oswald's. By the look she received from the judge, she realized that he would indeed be permitted to. "Well, no, but—"

"No physical evidence, $5,000,000 bail? That is an extreme injustice, Your Honor. The State cannot be permitted to treat citizens in such a way. I demand that Mr. Gutierrez be released on his own recognizance," Gary bellowed out while Ms. Sanders was mid-sentence. Ms. Sanders looked revolted by his rude behavior, but by looking at the judge, she realized that, rude or not, it was an effective tactic.

"Your Honor, we have several conversations recorded that have Mr. Gutierrez discussing the criminal operation with others that have been charged in this racketeering ring." The judge looked back at Gary, and Ms. Sanders returned to her usual smug look that made her look like a rather overfed pug.

"Were drugs or weapons discussed?" Gary said with a smile.

Ms. Sanders frowned. "We believe that they were working in codes. We believe horses meant meth and goats meant guns."

Gary smiled, knowing that, although Ms. Sanders believed she was being clever, he had just won the argument. "Your Honor, we don't deny the existence of such conversations. However, as I already presented in my brief to the court, Mr. Gutierrez is a horse trainer. He works on multiple farms in the Klamath area. He helps show horses, does general cowboy work, and even *negotiates* sales of farm animals."

He emphasized the last part. "The State has nothing, Your Honor. We ask for the release of an innocent man." He sat down slowly.

Judge Oswald frowned. "The charges did make it through grand jury, and they are serious A class felonies. Based on his lack of criminal history, I do not believe that Mr. Gutierrez is any sort of danger to the public or himself, but I must consider at the very least that being here with a green card and having strong ties to Mexico makes Mr. Gutierrez somewhat of a flight risk. I will set bail at $5,000. Mr. Gutierrez, you will have to have someone pay $500, 10 percent of the bail, to get a secure release at the jail." It was the first time that the interpreter speaking to Mr. Gutierrez really went noticed as Judge Oswald made sure to give the interpreter the proper time to explain this to Mr. Gutierrez.

"Thank you, Your Honor," Gary stated as he left the courtroom, not bothering to look at Ms. Sanders, who was giving him a look of great loathing. Gary was fairly sure that his client hadn't needed the interpreter, as he had been nodding at the right times during the argument. In the five minutes he had had with him in the court holding cell, Mr. Gutierrez had not spoken more than five or six words of English to him, but Gary could tell he was no fool. This case was going to be extraordinarily interesting.

As he was leaving the courtroom, three people got up from a bench and followed him out. "Thank you so *much*! I will be so glad to have my Eddie back at home," Ms. Gutierrez exclaimed while embracing Gary, and she began sobbing. The two other people Gary recognized as Ron and Gillian Greenburg. They were members of Eddie Gutierrez's church that owned a bakery downtown and a ranch about twenty miles out of town.

Ron Greenburg had salt-and-peppered hair. He was a tall man who walked with a certain sense of authority. He spoke with a very deep voice and rough handshake. Ron was at least twenty-five years the senior to Ms. Greenburg. She couldn't have been more than thirty-five. She was just under six feet tall with long auburn hair that touched her buttocks. She couldn't have weighed more than 110 pounds (before Mr. Greenburg had bought her the new breasts, which had to add thirty pounds by the look of them).

The most intriguing part of this was that Gary recognized that when Jane Gutierrez had handed him the $25,000 check to pay for his services, the name on the check read Ronald Greenburg. Ronald Greenburg obviously thought that Eddie Gutierrez was innocent . . . or at least that for some reason it was worth $25,000 to try to continue to keep him a free man. Gary made a mental note of this, as he did with all minor details. He had a funny suspicion that somehow or another, Mr. Greenburg was more involved than having sat in front of the Gutierrez family in church for a number of years.

"Of course, Ms. Gutierrez," Gary replied with a smile. He had tried to break the embrace at the standard two Mississippi count for hugs, but by fourteen Mississippis, he was still failing at his attempts. "Make sure to take the $500 up to the jail. When he gets out, he is to call my office right away to make an appointment. I want to see him either later this afternoon or tomorrow." He shook hands with Ron and Gillian after Ms. Gutierrez's embrace broke and moved to leave the courthouse.

"Hey, *fucker.*" Gary turned to look at who had called for him. A young blonde woman in a black dress pantsuit was approaching him. She had blue eyes framed by black plastic hipster glasses, chubby cheeks that framed the smile on her bulging lips well, and was about six inches shorter than Gary, who in his own right was vertically challenged. "Nice bullshittin' in there. I couldn't believe the look on that cunt Sanders's face when Ozzy set the bail! Ha!" She smacked him on the ass as she shouted the last word.

"Hey, Victoria, how did you do?" Gary replied conversationally. This was often how Victoria had greeted him. When she was drunk, she often tried more than smacking his ass. But as Gary was a faithfully married man, even if faithfully married didn't correlate to happily married, he didn't allow it to happen. Even men who are miserable in their marriages can take pride in saying they are faithful, he reflected.

"I think you softened her up. I thought my client was fucking fried. Two counts of racketeering and bail at $25,000. Although it just might be the length of the day for the judge. I have no idea what Sanders was thinking. I mean, I know the cunt is from the

Department of Justice, so she doesn't have a clue how Judge Oswald operates, but she couldn't have called a district attorney to see what happens in this Podunk county? She should have known you can't keep Rose in arraignments all day or she will start giving you weird rulings just to take the staleness out of the fucking day." She barked a laugh.

"I'm glad it worked out for your guy too. Maybe they are all innocent?" Gary snickered with a mischievous grin.

"Who cares as long as the checks clear, right?" Victoria laughed. Gary felt a tinge of annoyance at this. This kind of thinking always bothered him. There were enough stereotypes about how terrible lawyers are. Most of the world viewed him as a soulless life-sucking parasite. A lot of lawyers he knew, like Victoria for example, enjoyed this. They embraced it. He never had. In truth, he had never been in it for the money, but he actually enjoyed helping people. He had dreamed of getting acquittals of innocent men standing trial for murders. But mostly his job when he worked on criminal cases boiled down to trying to get actual criminals the least amount of jail time possible so that they could go back to their society's collapsing lifestyles as quickly as possible. Gary had to justify representing men accused of molesting children by saying that it was the person's rights that he was defending, not the person himself. That no matter what, when it boiled down to it, he was working for everyone's greater good. Keeping a balance that ensured that the government couldn't kick in your door whenever it pleased without actual evidence and making sure that everyone was given a proper trial and due process. But the faces of the innocent victims haunted Gary more than the idea of faceless souls being persecuted without cause.

When he worked with family law, he felt like an instrument that drove marriages apart. It was always even more awkward when a divorce client would come in with a story of a marriage that was better than Gary's own marriage. In truth, he felt like the job "attorney" should be classified in the same category as "hooker." He sold his beautiful mind every day to people who barely bothered to help themselves and helped others even less. Every day was an internal struggle between money and happiness. He would be happier teaching, or perhaps working as a doctor. With the money the career provided, his son never wanted for anything and never would. He would wear a purple dinosaur suit and dance around to children's songs all day if the money was good enough for his son's future. It wasn't that he didn't *love* parts of his career. Every job had its ups and downs. But days like today simply were heavy on his soul.

"Ya, I guess you're right about that," Gary replied, coming out of the haze of his internal monologue. He had neither time nor the patience to have a philosophical argument with Victoria Wampach at the moment.

"So what do you have going on this afternoon, sweet cheeks?"

Sweet cheeks? He was often called this by Victoria, although he couldn't figure out why. Outside of the simple fact that he could not understand why women found male butts appealing at all, he often felt awkward when anyone made a comment about his appearance, good or bad. That is not to say he wasn't a confident man. He felt he was somewhat average-looking. He didn't find himself to be grotesque at least. He was fairly vertically challenged, reaching maybe five and half feet tall. He had brown hair, dark-chocolate-brown eyes, a rather large pointy nose, and long cheekbones. He was slender but not in much shape as he had blown out his left knee playing high school soccer and had not been able to exercise properly in several years. At least, he had told people it was from soccer. In truth, he tore it falling up his stairs at an apartment his freshman year in college. His confidence came from his mind, not his looks. His confidence developed later on in life, as Gary the lawyer sounded a lot better than Gary the politics nerd.

"I got to consult with a new family law client. Custody, I think. It's been a pretty fucked-up day already. Hopefully, it isn't too heavy," he replied as they walked down the street toward their separate offices. "It has been nice talking to you, Victoria. I'll see you later."

"Bye, fucktard," she said by way of a goodbye.

Gary walked into his office, a small lime-green-painted house that had been converted to an office space decades ago. After he made his way down the short hall, he was greeted by his receptionist, "Hey, Gary, how did it go?"

"Awesome," Gary replied. "Five-thousand-dollar bail. That check cleared, right? When is my appointment?"

"Fuckin' A. It's in about five minutes. Check should clear by Friday. Can I get you anything?" she asked.

"No, I'm good, I'm just going to sit in my office for a few minutes and gather my thoughts. Page me when she is here."

His receptionist was not someone you would expect to have working in a law office, at least on the outside. Marti Wood had short blond hair and tattoos from her ankles to her neckline. She had several piercings, most of which Gary was convinced were in places he had never seen. She had a son named Peyton in prison for, of all things, picking up an ATM by himself when he was high and putting it in the back of a truck. He had never been able to open the ATM before he was arrested. She had a worse mouth than Victoria on most days, but unlike Victoria, she had enough sense to not swear around people until she got to know them. She had a wrinkled face from her several years of smoking and other recreational activities Gary had never asked her about. But she was loyal, quick-witted, and willing to help out with anything the office needed.

Gary closed his office door when he entered the room. It was a mid-sized office, with several paintings of ships on the wall. He hated them, but they looked the part of attorney office paintings, so he kept them up. He would have rather hung up posters of Pearl Jam and Metallica but thought that might not go well with incoming clientele. There was a large oak polished L-shaped desk in the room, with his computer on the shorter part. His desk chair was large, black, and had too much cushion for most people. There was a bookshelf with random books of law and various treatises he had collected. The two chairs for clients were incredibly unattractive hardwood chairs that looked rather like old dining room table chairs that had been bought at secondhand stores. In truth, they had, but since he had just opened his own office a couple months before, money was a bit tight.

When he sat down in his large office chair, he opened his desk drawer and took out a small wooden box and opened it. Three objects were inside: World War II dog tags that said "Gary Tornow" given to him as the namesake of his paternal grandfather, a picture of Gary and his son at the beach, and a small bottle of pills. He took a couple of aspirin from it with a bottle of water sitting on the desk.

"They are here, Gary," Marti shouted unnecessarily loud over the intercom.

"Just a second," Gary replied. He sniffed several times and took a tissue to wipe sweat from his upper lip. He adjusted his tie and took off his sports jacket to hang on the wall. He pushed the intercom on the phone. "You can bring them in now," he told Marti. About fifteen seconds later, she opened the door and led in four beautiful women and a man that looked a bit like a lumberjack. The man seemed a little out of place next to the women who had entered the office.

Three of them were clearly sisters and one the mother of the sisters. The youngest appeared to be barely out of high school but was carrying an infant no older than a month in a car seat, and the eldest couldn't have been over twenty-five. The mother was young to have daughters of such an age. She had blond hair; Gary thought it must be dyed as all the daughters sported brunette hair. She had green eyes and a kind, soft face, with the exception of a faint scar that went from the upper left side of her forehead down to the bottom right of her cheek. The scar went across her nose; it almost looked like the scar of a slashing motion, although it was not deep. Her nose was also slightly crooked, as if it had been broken badly before and reconstructed. She was short. She was not heavyset per se but had the look of a woman whose weight wavered back and forth from time to time and was probably about forty pounds over her eldest daughter's weight at the moment. She had pearly white teeth that almost appeared fake. She was still gorgeous, but Gary could tell that at one point she was absolutely stunning. Either years or more likely a tragedy of some sort, as he took note of her scar, had robbed her of a great deal of beauty.

He introduced himself first to what appeared to be the eldest of the daughters. He had the suspicion based on her age and the matter that they were there for, custody of a three-year-old child, that she would be his client. "Hi, I'm Gary. It's nice to meet you," he said, warmly.

"I'm Katelyn Gail, nice to meet you. This is my mother, Jerry; my sisters, Lucy and Caroline; and my fiancé, Joey." She smiled as she said this. She had long dark hair that ran to her butt. She had warm dark eyes and a beautiful round face. She had shallow cheekbones and a short nose. Her smile was beautifully intoxicating. She was short and slender but with wide hips of a mother. Her teeth were as white as her mother's, but he could tell from the slight crookedness of the bottom row that they were genuine. She wore a hot-pink short-sleeved shirt, jeans, and cowgirl boots.

He looked around the room and shook hands with them all in turn. "It is nice to meet you all. Please sit down." Marti had brought three more chairs from the lobby into the room.

The man, Joey, looked like he would have rather been anywhere else in the world. He had a large beard and was wearing a flannel shirt. His jeans were dirty, caked with dirt in some spots. The middle sibling, Caroline, was as stunning as her elder sister, if not more. They shared many traits. Her hair was also long but was a light brown, not dark. Her face was longer than her sisters. Caroline had slim hips and large breasts, which, judging by the black V-cut shirt she was wearing, she prided herself on. She looked about six to eight inches taller than her sisters and mother, but on second glance, Gary noticed she was wearing large heels under her jeans. She smelled like a mixture of finger nail polish and cigarettes.

The youngest sister, Lucy, was looking at the small child in the car seat with glowing love. It must be hers, he thought, as he observed the young woman. Like her sisters, she was glowing with beauty. She had her family trait of the long hair to her buttocks. It was dark, like Katelyn's, but she had put four streaks of hot pink in it. Her eyes, like her sisters, were dark brown. Her lips were beautifully plump. Her face was slender, and her nose slightly longer than her sisters' noses. She was skinnier than either of her elders by at least twenty pounds, but perfectly proportioned nonetheless. She was wearing a black skirt, white V-cut blouse, and gray leather boots up to her knees with several straps on them.

He had an odd feeling as he looked at the woman, a nervous feeling. He rarely felt nervous about anything at all anymore, the least of all anything to do with a woman barely out of high school. Something poked at him, but he couldn't put his finger on it as he admired her beauty. He then realized that, although not more than a few seconds, he had likely been starting too long at the youngest sister. "Um, so, Katelyn. What can I help you with today?"

"Where do I begin?" asked Katelyn shyly.

"Tell me everything from the beginning, not bits and pieces. Tell me like you are reading a book to me chronologically," Gary recited.

"Well, I have a son. He is three. His name is Brandon. I had him about a year after high school. I had been dating this guy named Paul, and we got pregnant. He is an EMT. Me and him were sort of serious, but the baby sort of escalated that relationship faster than it needed to be. We were going to get married . . . and when the wedding day came, I . . ."

"Didn't show up," her mom finished her sentence as Katelyn seemed lost on how to describe the situation. Gary had that sense that the mother's words came with a lot of weight behind them. He wasn't sure if this was due to the mother being mad about Katelyn leaving Paul on the day of the wedding, a prediction that she always knew it was going to happen in a similar fashion, or some other motherly meaning.

"Well, ya," Katelyn continued. "Up until about one year ago, Paul had only every other weekend with Brandon. I have been giving him some extra time in the summer along with the weekend time. I try to accommodate Christmas and stuff like that."

"Go on," Gary said, nodding as he jotted notes down on his legal pad.

"Anyways," Katelyn continued, "now he wants fifty-fifty time. We brought the paperwork I was served with." Katelyn reached into her purse and could not seem to find the paperwork. Her youngest sister, Lucy, rolled her eyes at her sister, reached into her infant's diaper bag, and pulled out the papers, then began admiring her infant again.

Gary took the paperwork from Katelyn and examined it. It was standard, asking for fifty-fifty time, the direction that the State's laws had led them to. It was likely he was going to get the fifty-fifty time, he thought as he read the papers. It was the norm, and if Paul was a minimally adequate parent, then Gary couldn't see a way out of it. But somehow he knew that this client would not be very accepting of that.

Before he had to make his decision on how to delicately tell her this fate, the youngest sister spoke. "Victoria already told you that he would get the fifty-fifty, Kate. You need to tell him about what Brandon has been saying. That is how this can be solved."

"Right. I had talked to this other attorney in town, Victoria Wampach, and she . . . well, it was odd. I had an appointment with her initially, and she talked me up. She made it sound like we were going to wipe the floor with Paul and there was no way he would get fifty-fifty. Then when I came back the next day to hire her, she kept going on and on about how hard it would be even though I had told her what Buggy has been saying."

Gary nodded. This was not the first time that he had heard of Victoria doing this. "Well, I'm sorry you didn't see her as being honest from the beginning, but she has the right of things in general. Fifty percent of the time for each parent is the norm nowadays. The laws don't favor mothers. The biggest things you have going for you is that you have been Brandon's primary caretaker for his whole life. You will maintain custody—meaning you can make major medical, school, and religious decisions—but that doesn't do much for you. Medical decisions that are optional don't come up a lot with healthy children. With the exception that Brandon will go to school in the school district you live in, assuming you and Paul live in different districts?" Gary asked. Katelyn nodded. "He would have the same right to inspect records, talk to teachers, visit him at school, etc. And as far as religious decisions, the State can't favor a religion. The only thing it does for religion that I have seen while practicing is that the custodial parent gets to decide if a child will be getting a circumcision or not." He frowned slightly at the disappointed look on Katelyn's face. "But if something is going on with Brandon at Paul's house, maybe I can do something."

She smiled, and the air seemed to blow back into Katelyn. "Well, I can't be certain this is going on. Mind you he is only three."

"He is the smartest three-year-old that I know," said Lucy. She looked at him intently. "Buggy keeps saying that Amy, who is Paul's fiancée, smacks him all the time. We can't get more than that out of him."

"Well . . ." said Gary, "that is something. But at three, that is going to be hard to get in to court. I can have you guys testify as to what you heard. There is a hearsay exception in the Oregon rules of evidence that allows for such testimony in situations that may involve child abuse." He paused at the puzzled looks to explain. "Hearsay means that normally statements made out of court and offered in court for the truth of the matter asserted by the statements are not admissible. They are seen as unreliable and would lead to even more 'he said, she said' controversy than we now have." He paused, thinking. "There may be a way though. What are your finances like?"

"Well, I have enough to pay you the $2,500 retainer your receptionist told me we would have to pay, but not much else. I am a student at the Klamath Community College and work part-time. The money is from my grandma." Katelyn had a grim look on her face when she said this.

"Okay then. Well, my advice is that if you don't hire me, hire someone. Child custody is a complex legal issue. But we need more." He looked at his computer and got a phone number from his directory. He wrote it down on the back of one of his cards and handed it to Katelyn. "Here, Steve Allen is a child counselor in town specializing in play therapy for younger children. I want you to contact him right away and get Brandon in."

"But I don't have insurance that will cover that for Brandon, and I don't have the mo—"

"You can pay me $1,500 for now. We will figure the rest out later," Gary cut in. "There is no reason to go to trial at all if we can't find more. Take the over $1,000 and get Brandon to Steve. If he tells Steve these things, we may have a case. Otherwise, we will probably settle and will likely not make it through the whole $1,500."

Katelyn looked as though she was about to tear up but pulled herself together. "Thank you so much," she replied.

He walked her through the retainer paperwork, took the check, gave her a receipt, and once again shook hands with all the family members.

The appointment had taken some time; it was already five thirty. Marti had gone home by the time Katelyn was ready to leave. Gary went back to his desk and pulled out his wooden box again. He didn't take any more pills but stared at the picture of his son before he ventured home.

CHAPTER 2

● ● ● ● ● ● ●

You Have the Conn

Gary's car rolled into the short driveway. He saw the lights on in the living room through the window, although heavy brown curtains allowed only glimpses of light. The porch light flickered on and off as the wind blew on the old light fixture.

The house was in a well-kept neighborhood on Hammock Street. It was a one-story house with a large partially finished basement. It was an older house painted in brown, with a fake brick finish on the bottom. The first floor was slightly elevated, and a large wood porch sat in the front of the house. There were three bedrooms in the house, although one of them was in the basement. Gary was rarely able to keep up with the yard and hired a neighbor boy to trim the bushes and mow the lawn during the summer. But as kids had gone back to school, the yard was not overgrown per se but looked rather unkempt. Gary had never felt at home in the house. He hadn't really felt at home in a long time.

He walked up to the stairs and onto the front porch. A sense of dread began to spread from his heart, pumping into every inch of his body as if it were moving through his veins. Gary opened the door to find a sight not unusual to him. His son, Sam, was sitting on a rug about a foot from the large television in the corner. The coffee table was riddled with dishes of all sorts: half-full cups, plates from breakfast and lunch, small empty chip bags, and granola bar wrappers. On the floor, toys appeared to lead a small line straight from Sam to his bedroom. A basket full of clean laundry sat on the couch. Gary assumed that Staci had meant to fold the laundry but got distracted as two towels were neatly folded next to the overflowing basket. Staci was nowhere to be seen.

Gary walked through and kissed Sam on the head, messing his hair up afterward with his hands. His son turned around and grabbed his leg. Sam held his arms up, gesturing to be held. Although three years old, Sam often did not like to speak. It wasn't that he couldn't. He had a rather large vocabulary for his age, especially as Gary would often read briefs out loud as Sam played for editing purposes. Gary would often watch Sam play with his toy fire trucks and directing traffic. Sam would be playing with his trucks and say words above his age level like *deposition, arraignment,* and *dissolution.* Gary would catch Sam using the words for a few days after the reading in the most peculiar of ways.

The truth was that Sam just didn't really need to talk. His mother would cater to him without him needing to speak, at least when she was in the room. He would talk about imaginary things or make small juvenile jokes about flatulence, but for the most part, he was silent except for when talking to himself.

Gary reached over and turned off the television. He began to gather the dishes and trash off the coffee table and floor. He threw the leftover food out with the rest of the trash, rinsed the dishes in the sink, and placed the dishes in the dishwasher.

Gary heard footsteps growing louder walking toward the kitchen from his bedroom. "Oh, good, you're home," Staci said, peeking her head around the corner. She had bleach-blond hair chopped to above her shoulders. It was partially Gary's fault that her hair was this way. One day when he came home from work, Staci had commented that she no longer liked her long red hair. Gary had stated that he loved her long hair. Staci asked if he would be upset if she cut it and dyed it blond. Gary had responded in what he thought was a sensitive and loving manner that he really, really loved the long red hair and that he thought it was beautiful. It was chopped off and dyed the next day. Staci was taller than Gary by about three inches. She was unnaturally skinny for her wide child-bearing hips. Her weight fluctuated continuously during their marriage, but in the last six months, it had landed on super skinny, mostly due to the fact that any meal Gary would cook for Staci would go uneaten.

She walked past him without any more acknowledgment of his existence other than the initial greeting. While passing, she kissed Sam on the forehead. For a moment, Gary thought about saying, "How was your day?" or "What are you doing?" Something to at least make the encounter slightly less awkward, but she was down the basement stairs before he could get the words out.

Gary brought a couple of Sam's toy fire trucks into the kitchen for Sam to play with as he cooked them dinner. As was custom, he made a plate for Staci and yelled down the stairwell to the basement that dinner was ready, and he shut the basement door again. The faint smell of marijuana that made its way up the stairs was too much for Gary to handle, especially with Sam at his feet.

Gary and Sam ate in a jubilant manner. Without a woman to control the conversation, there were plenty of elbow farts and spoons being stuck to noses. Some nights, Sam would simply look at his food and move it around to make it look like he ate. But somehow the small child always managed to eat like an elephant on spaghetti night. Or as Sam called it, s'getthi.

Gary cleaned up afterward and called Sam into the bathroom to wash before they winded down for the evening. After the bath, Gary poured milk into a small sippy cup for Sam, putting a small amount of chocolate mix in. Sam sat on Gary's bed in his underwear, sipping slowly at the chocolate milk. As was their routine, Gary offered Sam a set of his own pajamas to wear to bed and one of Gary's T-shirts. Sam pointed at the shirt, as he had for the two-hundredth-some-odd time in a row. Gary held Sam's hand as they went onto the couch. After lying down, Gary held Sam in his left arm with Sam's head on his chest. With his right hand, Gary used the television remote to find a show that he thought Sam would both enjoy and fall asleep to. He decided on a cartoon about a train station. Sam found the idea of the show exciting, but the thrills of commercial shipping only lasted for so long.

As Sam nodded off, Gary changed the channel to BBC America. With his son in his arms, he began to ponder the relative despair of his existence. His social life hinged completely on two beings: his three-year-old son . . . and Captain Jon-Luc Picard. Outside of his secretary, he couldn't think of another person whom he had a meaningful social connection to. Having your son as your best friend, Gary thought, was the greatest gift anyone could ever ask for. Having the only meaningful adult connection you had outside of the workplace be to a fictional *Star Trek* character was . . . he wanted to use the word *pitiful* but realized that he would have to apologize to the word *pitiful* if he did so.

Although he often hated aspects of his career, at the very least it was exciting. His life at work was thrilling. All day long he heard about gruesome crimes, horrific injuries, and could dwell on the issues of others' failed marriages instead of his own. He slowly drifted off as he watched the television.

He woke to the slow drip of chocolate milk onto his shirt. Sam was still asleep with his head on Gary's chest and his legs curled up to his stomach. Gary glanced over and saw the television playing an older version of *Doctor Who* that he didn't know. As *Star Trek* was over, Gary knew that it had to be sometime after 2:00 a.m. He picked up Sam and moved him into his bedroom. Although Sam was asleep, Gary sang him the same song he had sang to Sam every night since he was born.

"Hey, okay, we had another fantastic day, and now it's time to say . . . goodnight! 'Cause we got places to go, bubbles to blow, stories to share, and dreams to grow, so goodnight . . ." Gary covered Sam with his small ducks comforter, kissed him on the cheek, and plugged in Sam's night-light.

Gary slowly closed Sam's door, leaving it a sliver open. As he walked back into the living room, Gary heard whimpering from the heating vent coming from the basement. He stared at the vent for a few minutes or maybe ten minutes. He wasn't sure. He knew, more likely than not, she was fine. And that if he went down there to check, she was likely so high that he would have something thrown at him, he would be yelled at, or any number of other unpleasant things. After a rather loud gasp from the vent, he resigned himself to put up with whatever might be going on in the basement.

As he walked down the stairs, Gary noticed that all the lights were still on despite the late hour. He walked through the laundry room, into the finished side room. He saw Staci lying on the floor, her legs pushed up to her chest. Gary observed the scene. In the corner lay Staci's yoga equipment. It was neatly folded next to some weights and a treadmill. When Staci had asked Gary about having the basement finished, it was for a workout room, not this. He looked in the other corner to see a short object about as tall as a pop can. It was a bottom-rounded glass object. Gary thought it was a bong but was always corrected and told it was a bubbler if and when he did see the object.

His eyes moved to the small metal table in the center of the room. One of Staci's pill bottles lay on the ground, her pills spilling out of it. Gary reached down and picked up the bottle to examine it. It was Adderall. On the table lay what appeared to be about three pills crunched practically into dust. Little trails of dust were all over the table.

Gary noticed that Staci was rocking back and forth in the fetal position. "It's cold," Staci repeated over and over again.

Gary walked back upstairs and went into their room. He grabbed a large comforter and reached onto the bed and grabbed a pillow. He made his way back downstairs to Staci, finding her in the same state in which he left her. He gently picked up her head and placed it on the pillow. He took the blanket and laid it over her. He picked up the pills, the ones that were still whole, and placed them back in the pill bottle. He pocketed the pill bottle and turned around, heading back upstairs.

Every fiber of his being told him to flush the pills down the toilet. Every ounce of determination pushed him toward it. But . . . he took the pill bottle out of his pocket and placed it in the medicine cabinet. He spent a few minutes tidying up the kitchen sink area despite the late hour as it bothered him when too much stuff was laid on the sink. He brushed his teeth and made his way back to the couch.

It had been this way ever since Sam was born. It started with post-partum depression, and it warped into something much more.

Staci's father had always struggled with his mental health, but Gary hadn't thought much of it until now. Her behavior was sporadic. She threw things, hit things, yell, scream whenever she got truly upset. Gary had always been able to calm her down. She would always say dramatic things when she was mad like "I'm going to murder you" or "I hope you die." She would apologize later, and he never thought much of it. But as her behavior became more sporadic, Gary worried that someday she could snap. Help needed to come soon, and he wasn't sure how to get it. His mind grew tired with the burdens of his marriage weighing him down.

Gary opened the DVR list on the television and absentmindedly picked a *Star Trek* episode he had probably watched fifty times. He grabbed a blanket from the same closet he had before and grabbed another pillow from the bed. He placed them on the couch and relaxed, trying to simply forget that for all the talks he had with drug abusers, and more important the families of drug abusers, he himself was an enabler. Not because he ever approved of the marijuana, Adderall, Vicodin, or any number of things that made their way into his basement, but because the idea of ever having to be without Sam for a night was unbearable. Further, he knew that Staci, being a stay-at-home mother, would greatly damage his chances of having a majority of the time with Sam even if she was an abuser as it was so hard to prove things in court.

Their relationship hadn't started out of poetic romance or any cute story. It had sprung out of convenience and booze, as relationships often do. Gary now had a great job and made great money. Armed with a prestigious career, Gary knew he would have prospects, but outside of the piece of paper in his office that read "Juris Doctorate," he never felt very good about himself. He loved that he was smart but always felt that he would have given up 20 IQ points to be at least average-looking. But before this piece of paper, Gary had very little in the ways of enticing a woman.

Years ago in college at his friend Preston's house, Preston's little sister had begun to drink with Preston and his friends, one of them being Gary. As the night passed, Gary became increasingly drunker than the others. Not because he drank more, but because he was at least six inches shorter than the others and thirty pounds lighter. When his friends had all decided that they would stroll down the street for more beer, it was democratically concluded that Gary was too drunk to go, so he was to stay home with Preston's little sister Staci and, well . . .

Their entire relationship had been convenience from the point forward. The student body president at Portland State University, working a full-time job on the side, and attempting to keep up with an academic schedule to get him into law school made it so Gary had little time for a social life. While Gary was going to college, Staci was a waitress at a small diner. She would come home and smoke pot all night, but Gary was too busy to care much. She was conveniently unobtrusive. After college, they were married mostly because Gary had promised they would be married before he went to law school. In law school, there was even less time to be together. And then Staci was pregnant with Sam. After passing the bar and waiting for employment, Staci and Gary had the only extended amount of time with each other that they had had since they began their relationship six years before. Now they were at nine years together, five years married. How do you spend almost a decade with a person and never truly grow close to them?

It wasn't that they hadn't had good times. In nine years, you accidently slip into fun on occasion. They had some television shows they had watched together and some games they played together. But each "together" item was often short-lived, and even when they were doing things together, Gary would notice Staci taking frequent breaks to go into their bedroom. Although she always denied it, a faint smell of marijuana always gathered around one of the windowsills that had blackened marks from what Gary had assumed were burns from a lighter.

He still cared about her but not in the sense that a husband should love a wife. More like someone would care for a cat or a goldfish. It wasn't that love had never been there, but any trace amounts were on life support. The love that had been there, Gary realized, was more dependence than love. Staci depended on him in almost every fashion. She was completely financially dependent on him. Socially, her anxiety was so bad that Gary had to do all the shopping and even had to schedule her doctor appointments for her. Gary depended on Staci to simply be there so he wouldn't be alone. But that use had all but been extinguished months ago.

Hollywood always made love look so . . . perfect. Beautiful people, always in love, always in heat, and always passionate. Beautiful? Gary never was. Staci had been to a degree, but her own self-image issues pushed her down a path that robbed her of beauty. Love? They hadn't said that word in a while. Heat? Intimate touching was now a contest to see how many times someone could say, "You're doing it wrong." Passion? He knew passion from the drive he had in his career. He had never had that drive with Staci.

He continued to watch the show and slowly began to feel his eyes droop under the weight of his thoughts.

Slowly light began to flood the room once more. He was sitting on throne in a large marble stone room. In front of him lay a variety of fruits on stone table carved with ancient runes. Several leather draping in the room were painted with a large picture of a leafless ash-white tree.

Singing entered and exited his dreams rapidly. About ten feet from the table stood a very small man. Long blond locks and stocky stature, the man's eyes were the color of seawater. The man was the source of the singing. Outside of the walls and the song, he heard the cries of souls leaving cold bodies.

The man's voice . . . it was beautiful but eerie. The halfling's voice was not that of a man but a woman. A familiar voice. Punctured early and often by short spurts of playful giggling and hysterical crying of a woman. It was the high pitch and enchanting cry of a harpy, muddled with the song of the sirens and the lyrics of . . . Gene Wilder?

"Come with me . . . and you'll beeeeeee . . . hehehehe . . . in a woooooooooooooorld of pure imagination . . . Take a look, and you'll see into your imagination . . ." Violent sniffling and sobbing began to occur and carry into the next lines.

"We'll . . . begin . . . with a spin, traveling in the world of my creation . . . What we'll see will defy explanation." The room was shaking slightly. Or at least it felt that way as his head gently bobbed. The laughter grew louder.

Joy poured into the words. "If you want to view paradise simply look around and view it. Anything you want to, do . . . *it*." The final words, emphasized loudly, snapping his head back violently in shock and awaking him from his deep slumber.

Dimly, Gary saw an infomercial in the background as his eyes were still partially closed. He never understood how oxygen could make laundry so clean.

"There is no life . . . I know . . . to compare . . . with pure . . . imagination." Sobbing grew louder. His body moved slightly up and down as the body at his feet trembled.

Gary did not dare to look up and alert her to the fact that he was awake. He kept his eyes partially closed, watching for her shadow, waiting for her to move. But she just trembled on the edge of the couch, sobbing and giggling periodically. "Living there . . . you'll be free, if you truly . . . wish . . . to . . . be . . ."

The singing stopped, but sobbing and sobbing alone took over. It may have been five minutes or ten, or it could have been years. Gary lay still, feeling her eyes upon him.

Gary felt the couch lift as she stood. He heard Staci's footsteps head toward the bathroom. He saw the light come on from the hallway. Gary opened his eyes, knowing she was nowhere to be found at this point. He heard a loud clink, like a metal object hitting the floor. Sobbing grew louder and louder. The light remained off, yet he heard loud footsteps thunder from the bathroom to their bedroom. He heard the bedroom door open and slam violently.

Gary waited for the clock on the cable box to pass five thirty, about twenty minutes after Staci had stampeded into the bedroom. He got up and walked toward the bathroom, readying himself to shower as he didn't feel he could sleep anymore. He could still feel her eyes watching him.

He clicked the bathroom light on. The shower curtain rod was lying on the floor. Water was still in the bath, soapy with remnants of what appeared a bubble bath. He saw water on the floor. Even sober, she wasn't very good at keeping water off the floor. His eyes then fell to the clean sink area, or rather what was the clean sink area. He saw a large serrated hunting knife, unsheathed from the leather case, lying on the floor. Gary picked up the knife in a towel and headed toward the backdoor. He opened the trash can and threw it in.

CHAPTER 3

● ● ● ● ● ● ●

On a Scale of 1 to 10, How Shameful Is the Pornography You View?

Thoughts of the long night lingered in Gary's mind. Over and over again, the night played in his head. It wasn't a unique experience by any means, but it was a mixture of many nights he had experienced, as if all the horrors decided that they needed to be played out in one night. He had sensed Staci watching him before, but she was always quiet. She never spoke, just watched. This time, though, it had escalated. Why? His logical mind tried to explain the situation, but it couldn't. It was a boiling point, perhaps, where the water simply went over the sides of the pot. The situation kept getting worse and worse until it climaxed last night. At least he hoped it had climaxed.

Even in the lobby, where he sat alone with his thoughts, the smell of the county jail was rooted in his nose. It was faint, but nonetheless present. A mixture of sweat, semen, urine, and bleach. Thoughts of the smell gave him a headache. Today, it would be worse than normal. He would be in booking, which included an extra-strong urine and puke smell coming from cells with those that were still drunk from the night before.

When he gotten to his office that morning, he had received a voice mail from a frantic mother. "My son was arrested, and I don't really understand the charges. He is telling me that he is in for something different than the cops are saying." Shame about one's charges was often an indicator of guilt. Innocent men charged with a crime

40

would at least tell someone honestly what the allegations were. Gary did not have high hopes that this man was innocent. Gary was not even sure he could pay him. Sex abuse 1 charges usually meant a fee of at least $25,000 up front.

"Gary, you're up, dude," one of the guards called. The guard, nicknamed Tat, always wore long-sleeved shirts, even on days when it ventured above ninety degrees like today. Another attorney had noticed him at the store, and he was covered from shoulder to wrist in tattoos.

The guard led him through the doors and down a short hallway. As they turned to the right, the strong urine smell violated Gary's nostrils.

The room he was visiting turned out to be near the very end of a long hallway. Tat unlocked the door, opened it, and gestured Gary in. It was a familiar sight. As he was still in booking, the man still had the clothes he was wearing at the time of his arrest on. The man had neatly cut gray hair, large round spectacles framing green eyes, and was wearing a yellow polo shirt and jeans. There was no smell of alcohol or urine in this room, at least nothing that appeared to be from this particular room. So the damage he had done to his appearance must have been a result of being upset, not drunk. Wet streaks rolled down the man's cheeks. The polo shirt was drenched in what appeared to be tears, mixed with vomit. He apparently worked himself into such a frenzy that he threw up. The man was much, much older than Gary had expected. By the phone call, Gary expected a man in his twenties, not fifties. A fifty-plus-year-old mama's boy, the chomo glasses, and the fact that the man was obviously a coward all screamed guilt.

"My name is Gary Tornow. Your mother called and asked me to come speak to you." It was as waste of air to tell someone in booking at the jail "Good morning." "Before we begin, I don't want to know any details about what may or may not have—"

"I'm innocent!" the man blurted out, beginning to shake.

"Please, let me finish. As I was saying, I don't want to know any details about what may or may not have happened. I don't want to know because I have an obligation to report if I have evidence that client is lying while testifying. It you tell me facts at this stage, it could be hurtful to you later. I also want to remind you that this conversation is confidential. Don't share details of it with anybody. Next, make sure that everyone you talk to in the outside world, via phone, mail, etc., hears nothing about your case. If you make bail, you don't talk to anyone outside of here about it, okay?"

The man shook his head nervously.

"What is your name?" Gary clicked his pen and began to take notes.

"Robert. Robert Murray." The man was looking at the wall, blankly.

"Okay, Robert, so here is what we are going to talk about. We have three things we need to cover. I need to know what you have been accused of *but* not from your perspective of what happened. I need to know exactly what is being alleged. Second, I want to talk to you about the penalties involved with the crimes you have been arrested for. Third, we will talk about how much my representation costs and what it means." The man nodded slowly.

"So let's start from the beginning," Gary said calmly. "Tell me what the police told you about the arrest."

A bad idea, apparently. The man was not understandable with the loud sobs coming from his hands. "They . . . they . . . are saying that my . . . my . . . my grandson has accused me of molesting him. And I never—"

"Wait, I don't want to know if you did or not. In fact, that is immaterial to what I can do." Gary's stomach turned with self-loathing. "I just need to know what it is I am defending you against."

"Okay, okay . . ." The man nodded, his eyes glazed, staring at the wall. "My grandson, he is five. Well, step-grandson. My wife, it is her daughter's son."

"Do you have any children of your own?" asked Gary, assuming the answer. A man that had to be in his late fifties with no children was also a classic sign in this case. Robert shook his head side to side.

"Well, we were visiting them in Bonanza. They have a fairly small house. Adam's room is upstairs, and so is his parents'." Robert paused, taking a deep breath after almost sentence as if it caused him great agony. "Natalie, their daughter, she's about two, sleeps in the same room as the parents. Downstairs there is a small kitchen, a bathroom and a living room. So my wife and I were going to be sleeping in the living room. There is a hide-a-bed couch in there. We had it pulled out." Robert continued to take deep breaths, trying to work himself through the words.

"Go on," Gary said, waiting to sense a lie.

"Well, it was late, probably about ten. Adam's parents had gone to bed with Natalie. Sylvia, my wife, had dozed off on the hide-a-bed, so Adam and I were sitting at the foot of the bed. He had picked out a movie, *Scooby Doo* of some sort. It was a hot night, so I just was in my pajama bottoms. Adam was wearing a long shirt. So, well, usually Adam and I are very close. And we were joking around, and I reached over and tickled his tummy. Barely touched him." Gary saw the first lie in Robert's eyes. "And . . . and he just started yelling. Yelling that I had touched his penis. Sylvia woke up and just had this look of shock of her face. I started hearing his parents wake up, and they ran down the stairs."

One lie, that he just tickled him. Gary was no super genius that could detect lies by any means, but listening over and over again to suspects gave him a great understanding of human tendencies.

Gary pondered the situation. It *was* defendable. He had gone into more detail than Gary liked, but this was a fact-friendly accusation. But then why the accusation? Something felt off, as if maybe many events had been passed off as innocent, leading to this moment. Why the panic in the child? Had his parents told him that if someone, or specifically Robert, had touched his privates he was to scream right away? The man had reached over and tried to pass off a terrible crime as an innocent gesture. But Gary wondered, what else would be found?

"Okay. So basically, there was innocent tickling nothing else. Had you ever been with the child in a compromised position? I mean, had you given him baths, changed his diaper . . ."

"Of course," Robert interrupted, "I'm his grandfather. I've done all those things."

"Had you ever been accused of inappropriate behavior before?" Gary inquired.

"No, no, of course not." Another lie. There was a small stutter caught in the man's throat that had not manifested itself until this point. Robert wouldn't admit to it. None of them ever did. Robert appeared to be the typical uncle that hugged a little too long, stared a little too long, possibly make inappropriate comments about a developing child, and just put off a bad aura. Someone would say something. Depending on what it is, Gary likely could combat it.

"Okay, so what do you do for a living?"

"I'm an IT guy," Robert answered. He was so quick when he was telling the truth. So confident. It was amazing what honesty could do.

"So you work with computers. Robert, I have to ask, not because I think there is anything but because if there is, I want to do something sooner rather than later about it to try to get ahead of the issues," Gary said with some degree of rigor to his words. "You were picked up yesterday. Right now, the police are likely going to a judge and attempting to get a warrant to seize your computers. Given the nature of the crimes you are accused of, the warrant will be granted." He paused to let this set in. "So I need to know if there is even the *slightest* possibility that you have any underage pornography stored on your computers or if you have ever gone to a website that has had underage pornography on it."

"No, no, of course not. I mean, my wife and I use pornography as part of our sexual life, and you know, stuff pops up sometimes that might be odd, but nothing outside of that," Robert stated in a very matter-of-fact manner.

"What do you mean it just pops up?" Gary was a lonely married man. He understood what perusing for pornography meant. But not once had anything questionable ever popped up. Years ago, Gary had had a school librarian who put this issue into clear perspective every time a client made a statement of this nature: "The problem with computers is that they do exactly what you tell them to do." The distant memory rang through the years.

"Well, you know, pop-up ads and stuff. Just stuff like that. My wife, she will tell you," Robert said, trying to do so with confidence but too quickly to be reassuring.

"So every time you looked at pornography, it was with your wife? Never alone?" Gary said this with too much skepticism in his voice, but there was no way not to.

"I mean," Robert started, "I guess, I guess, well, not always, no. If she was out of town or something." Robert noted this. If something showed up that was troubling, when it was viewed would be pivotal. He didn't believe him either way, but it was his job to pursue all the issues.

"Speaking of your wife, how is she handling this?"

"I haven't talked to her since I was arrested. But this happened a few weeks ago, and she told me she believed me. I don't know now, but I hope so. I love her." Robert really did love her, Gary thought. The man's eyes were full of love for her. Gary noted this—not because whether he loved his wife or not would matter but because he would need to carefully explain to the wife what was going on if Robert ever had to plead. She may even need her own attorney. If Gary was able to negotiate a deal with little to no punishment, he would probably recommend it, given the serious nature of the charges. Robert's wife would likely have to be on board with him, accepting liability for a crime he did not commit.

"Okay, well, we need to talk about the process," Gary pushed forward. "It looks like Judge Oswald set your bail at $100,000. That means that you will need to have someone come down and post $10,000 to be granted a security release. Given the nature of your charges, you won't be allowed to be in places were minors normally congregate, and you can't be around minors. That means you can't go to bowling alleys, movie theaters, arcades, etc."

"What if I went to a really late movie?" Gary interrupted.

"Well, here is the issue there. Rated R movies mean under-17 restriction. That means that it is possible that children under the age of eighteen are present. That is not to mention that people overage could take minors into those movies. If it is really, really late, you still have the possibility. It is better to be safe than end back up here."

Robert nodded. "But it isn't just places that are obvious. You can't go to the grocery store for—"

"I can't go . . ." Robert interrupted. Gary held a finger up.

"Just let me finish. You can't go to the grocery store because minors are likely to be there, practically at any time. You need to have your wife do the shopping. An inconvenience but not impossible," Gary finished.

Robert sat there and appeared to ponder Gary's words. "Okay, so my wife, she works for a school. I usually go and help out, putting up decorations and stuff. Can I . . ."

"No," Gary stated abruptly. This was going to be a lot more difficult that he originally thought. This was a thick person. Or at least a person unwilling to accept the boundaries that were set before him. Robert would likely struggle to comply with his security release. "A school, at all times, is off limits."

Gary continued forward. "So here is the next part. This kind of charge is going to require a vigorous defense. My retainer, that is my cost, is going to be $25,000 pretrial. That covers all negotiations, investigations, etc. If we have not settled the case or had the case dismissed, I will need an additional $25,000 before a trial. These are flat fees. It doesn't matter if I spend five hours or five thousand hours, it is the same either way." Gary pulled out some paperwork, and Robert and Gary began to go through it.

They went through the paperwork quickly. Robert said that his mother would come post the bail. He didn't want his wife to have to be involved in any way.

On the drive back to the office, Gary thought about what it was that he would be going through at the office. A few minor appointments, but nothing too complicated. It wasn't the day that haunted him; it was what would happen tonight and if he was able to survive another night of . . . of . . . whatever the hell that was.

He pulled into the parking lot and saw that Marti's car wasn't in the parking lot. He thought about the day. Wednesday. That meant that Marti's granddaughter was getting out of school early. Marti usually took off early on Wednesdays.

Gary walked into the office and went through his voice mails. A couple of calls on negotiations, a marketing call, and a voice mail from a recent client he had recently retained, Katelyn Gail. "Hi, Gary, so I know we have court next week. I need to talk to you about a couple of issues that we didn't really get to go into last week. Things about my family's past that my ex, Paul, knows about. My family, well, we don't deal with the past well, and I, well, I think this could hurt me. Please give me a call back so I can come in and talk to you."

CHAPTER 4

● ● ● ● ● ● ●

Have a Drink on Me

"Please, have a seat." Gary gestured for Katelyn to take a seat. Unlike last time, she was alone. Before, she seemed to have an aura of a defeated person. Gorgeous, with her ebony hair and deep dark eyes, yet defeated, beaten down. She was wearing a pink tank top and tight jeans. Now she seemed surer of herself, as if she had made some sort of decision. Perhaps, Gary thought, he was about to learn why. She had a seat but did not speak.

"Okay, so tell me, what is on your mind? Obviously, having all your family here the first time may have made it difficult for us to openly discuss some of the issues that have been going on," Gary began.

"So here's the deal," Katelyn started, "my mother has been raising us all, me and my siblings I mean, alone for a while now." Gary had noted no mention of a father or father figure during their previous encounter. Katelyn was breathing heavily now, her eyes not fixated on Gary but at a point just beyond his left shoulder. Katelyn staring at the wall pushed Gary to dive for more information.

"Where's your dad in the picture?" Gary asked.

"Never met him," Katelyn said, shrugging her shoulders. "My mom got pregnant with me in high school and has never told me who it is. But . . ." Katelyn hesitated, "knowing Mom, I'm not sure she even knows who it is. Basically a broken-condom child." The defeated aura returned to Katelyn, but only temporarily.

"Anyways," Katelyn continued, "my stepdad, Donald, well . . ." Katelyn looked about the room, stumbling for words. "He is in prison. He tried to kill my mom. He beat her within an inch of her life."

This revelation was noteworthy but hardly worth the meeting today. Either way, Gary noticed no increase in breathing rate, tears, or any other emotional reaction during this story. The critical point, it appeared, was still to come.

"Let me look up the case." Gary turned toward the computer and began to search for the information on the Oregon Justice Information Network when he realized that Gail was not likely her stepfather's last name. "What is Donald's last name?" Gary asked.

"Murray," Katelyn answered. She put her elbows on her knees and placed her face in her hands for a moment. Although the high point had not been hit, it seemed this still wasn't easy to talk about.

Three cases appeared in the county. The first one, a disposition of guilty for attempted murder, assault with a deadly weapon, false imprisonment, and resistance of arrest. A twelve-year prison sentence accompanied this matter. The other two cases, filed around the same time, were . . .

"Is your middle initial *M*?" Gary asked, noting the initials of the victims, KMG and CMG.

"Yes." Katelyn was still looking at her hands.

"And your sister Caroline's is the same?"

"Yes, both *M*," Katelyn replied.

Katelyn's cause for concern became apparent to Gary rather quickly. "So Caroline and you were victims of sex abuse from Donald?" Gary asked, corresponding the initials of the second victim with the initials of one of Katelyn's sisters.

"I never wanted to talk about it," Katelyn sighed and continued, looking into Gary's eyes for the first time in about five minutes. "After Donald was arrested, Caroline told our grandma what he had done to her. Grandma took Caroline to see our mom, and she didn't believe it at first. Our grandma told the police because Mom was in the hospital still. They brought all the kids in to talk to the police first, and they asked each of us if we had anything we wanted to add. That's when I told them that it had been happening to me too."

Gary understood why Katelyn would believe that her being a victim of sex abuse would be significant to her case. In truth, statistics showed that almost one out of every three women had been exploited in some way during their childhood, a statistic well known to judges. No judge would find enough relevance to even allow a question about a litigant being a sex abuse victim.

Katelyn continued, "We went the next day to this place called CARES. They were really nice, but I wasn't ready to talk. I gave half-truths. I told them that he did things like flip my cheerleading skirts up and do things like rub against me. I wasn't ready to be honest." Now Katelyn began to choke back tears, one of which broke through the barrier and began to slowly drip down her right cheek. "I had to do horrible things to him. He made me do everything that he could except actual sex until Caroline must have been old enough for him to abuse. He never touched me after I went through puberty. He tried sex, but I was too small, and he would get frustrated and do other things."

"You told Paul all this?" Gary asked and already knew the answer. Had she not told Paul, it wouldn't be an issue. Gary pushed the box of tissues toward her.

"Thanks." Katelyn took one of the tissues. "Yes, I loved him. We were going to get married. I had never felt like that with anyone before. Paul took away the pain. I was able to do things with Paul I can't even do with Joey. It's like the pain came back."

"Like what, for example?"

"Well, I can't be intimate in the shower. I just can't. Until I was eleven, Donald took showers with me and . . ." The barrier holding back the tears burst, and Katelyn began sobbing loudly.

Gary moved from his side of the desk to the chair next to Katelyn. He placed a consoling hand on her right shoulder. "Katelyn, thank you for sharing this with me. I want you to know that I do not think that what you have told me will have any impact on your case."

Katelyn nodded but sobbed louder. It took about a minute to calm her down. "I know that, but there is more." There was a solemn look in Katelyn's eyes as she peeked at Gary, her makeup running down her cheeks. "When I left, they told me that there was enough from me to press some charges, sex abuse 3 I think, not anything major. They couldn't prosecute the case at all, though. Caroline was young, a young teenager. And our mom had a real hold over her. The police shouldn't have let us go home that night. By the time that the prosecutor got a hold of the information Caroline gave, it had my mom all over it, and they decided not to push forward after charging him. They said my mom had tampered too much with the evidence. I guess Caroline kept saying that 'I don't really know what happened, because what I do think I remember Mom says it didn't happen that way.' She didn't elaborate after that."

Gary put some thought into that. Gary knew from their previous discussion that Katelyn's mother had been Brandon's babysitter while Katelyn worked. Had Paul known that Jerry had given false information to a victim before, he could use this to his advantage. This was a huge blow if they wanted to get anything meaningful out of Brandon. Gary's brain turned over and over, brewing ideas. But something was bothering Gary when he realized there was significant hole in the logic.

"Why ask her to lie though? Why not have her tell the truth. These things happened. They happened to you. Why create lies about them and risk not being able to prosecute. Did your mom think that there wasn't enough? That Caroline might end up not telling enough?" Gary inquired.

Katelyn looked at Gary with complete composure for the first time during the meeting. "No, I think our mom was afraid that the whole truth would get out."

"The whole truth?"

"Look, I just don't have another babysitter for Brandon, and as terrible as it may seem, I only have my mom in this world. She may be a boil on the ass of humanity, but she is the only mom I have and . . ." Katelyn paused, hesitated for a few moments, and began with the same conviction and composure she started her explanation with. "I told Paul the truth about everything. He was my person. And I think that now he can use what my mom knew against me, especially since she really does have Brandon more than I do."

"What did she know?" Gary asked, fearing the worst.

"Everything," Katelyn responded without hesitation.

"How?"

"I was probably ten, about five years before Donald went away . . . I'm not even sure if he had touched my sister at this point. All her pain might have been avoided . . ." Katelyn's eyes drifted out of focus. Her face was morose as the pain was etched in it.

"Katelyn?"

She shook her head slightly, not acknowledging Gary had said anything. "I was in the shower with Donald. He left the bathroom door open, I think to hear if anyone got home. He . . . he had his fingers inside of me, my . . ." Katelyn continued without further elaboration as Gary nodded.

"Your mom came home?"

"Yes. Apparently, my mom came home, and he didn't hear because he wasn't paying attention, or was too excited to notice or something. But anyways, it was late, like 9:00 p.m. Mom came in the bathroom to brush her teeth, and neither of us noticed. He still had his fingers in me when mom opened the shower curtain, looking for her toothbrush. It was the first moment either of us noticed she was there. Donald had frozen, probably in fear, and his fingers were still inside of me when she looked. She grabbed her toothbrush, and I saw her . . ." Katelyn began to violently shake with tears going down her cheeks.

"What exactly did she see?"

"Everything. I saw her look right at him with his fingers still in me. She just shut the shower curtain and went to bed. I tried to talk to her about it the next morning, but I couldn't get the courage. She never brought it up." Katelyn looked flat, defeated.

"Did it ever happen again?" Gary didn't really need to know. But he felt this strange urge to talk to Katelyn. He knew that talking about issues would ultimately help victims, and he couldn't help but feel like he needed to help Katelyn.

"There were dozens of other times that she would walk into a super-suspicious scene and do nothing. I remember being naked in my parents' room. I don't even remember what he was doing to me or making me do to him, and Mom walked in. I remember he was a few feet from me, and he was . . ." Katelyn had tears all over her lap at this point; she sobbed through the last words. "He had an erection. And all that cunt had to say to him was that he needed to put it away because I shouldn't see it like that. I remember her taking me to Ross when I was like ten and her buying me a piece of lingerie and telling me to keep it in my drawers until I was ready to be a woman and Donald finding it and making me wear it for him. I wake up at night with images that I don't remember. Things I've blacked out. Things I just can't cope with. I don't even remember being touched by anyone but him, but I have dreams about my Uncle Bob touching me. We have all these pictures of a family trip to Hawaii when I was a kid, but I can't even remember getting on the plane. All I have are glimpses of things that happened. I remember images like blood swirling in water in a hotel shower. Most of all, though, I remember what happened right after Donald went to jail. The thing that still burns the most isn't the scars from having my innocence taken or having to do things to someone that was supposed to care about me. No, the thing that bothers me the most is the surprise my mom portrayed. The shock she made up in her face. The way she acted like a victim. The way she acted like she didn't have a clue. And the conviction she still has that she did everything she could when we were kids to be there for us." It was as if the faucet of Katelyn's revelations went from a slow drip to a heavy downpour as the last few sentences came in a rush, as if she had never been able to vent like that her entire life.

They sat in silence for a few minutes while they both gathered their thoughts. Gary looked up at the clock; it was half past three. It was the night that Staci generally took Sam to her friends to have a play date so Gary could go play poker. Gary looked at Katelyn during the silence. There was a beauty to her that he couldn't quite explain. It made everything more painful, much more painful than usual. There was always a struggle in all the cases Gary had that deal with sex abuse in one fashion or another. The cases themselves made his stomach churn, but they left it at that. This was different. This woman from head to toe was enchanting. The thought of her being hurt burned a fire within Gary, a fire he had never experienced. It tortured him. Gary couldn't explain to himself why the pain he had been told about by countless clients would all of a sudden break through with this woman. The morose nature of the topic itself was terrible enough. But to happen to her was a monstrosity.

"Where is Brandon at?" Gary broke himself out of the haze.

"With his dad this week." Katelyn monotone voice told Gary she had not snapped from the haze as quickly.

Gary pondered. He had never done this before with a client, but there was a connection in such a short span. And he couldn't kid himself. He needed a friend just as much as she did. "Let's go get a drink."

CHAPTER 5

● ● ● ● ● ● ●

Kiss from a Rose

Gary had a client who owned a bar just down the street, Whiskey's. He told Marti he was leaving early, and told her she could do the same. Katelyn had gone out to her car to grab a sweatshirt. Gary stood in the bathroom, looking in the mirror, pondering his decision. Gary hadn't gone out with a close friend in nearly three years, let alone an attractive woman whom he barely knew. He ran the cold water through his hands and rubbed his hands on his face. *It's just a drink . . . It's just a drink . . . It's just a drink . . .* he told himself over and over again.

Professionally, he knew he couldn't think about more than that, but his mind was tormenting him with images of what he could not partake in. This was ridiculous. Two minutes ago, this was an innocent moment, asking someone who needed a way to relax to join him for a drink. However, he knew better. Nothing was ever that simple. Now it seemed reckless, miscalculated, ill-conceived, unethical, and downright dangerous.

Gary opened the bathroom door, and Katelyn was waiting in the hallway. She had a faint smile on her face. She was wearing an Indianapolis Colts hoodie. Gary chuckled and smiled back. He took off his sports jacket, put it on the coat rack, and grabbed his Seahawks hoodie. "We might as well dress the same for the occasion."

Katelyn giggled. It was a genuine smile for once. "I thought you attorneys had to dress all dignified like all the time," she said in a mocking hillbilly voice.

"I'm not sure how dignified I'll be after a couple drinks. I haven't had a drink in . . ." It took Gary a moment to recall. "Probably since around the time my son was born."

They left his office and began walking toward the bar. "Don't worry, I'll teach you." Katelyn grinned at him. "You have a son? How old?"

"Three, about your son's age."

"Oh, where is he?" Katelyn asked.

"Um, with my wife." Gary's voice came out riddled with guilt, and he couldn't understand why.

"Ah, that's right." Katelyn blushed a bit. "So tell me about her."

Gary thought for a second. He wanted to say: *Well, she spends most of the day high. She listens to music all night long that not only do I not understand, but it scares the shit out of me. She stays at home with our son, and I am so concerned about him getting himself killed because she doesn't pay attention to him that I put him in daycare to give her a "break" a few times a week. I don't have anything in common with her anymore, and I'm not sure if I ever did or if I was just afraid of being alone. I should have left years ago, but we got pregnant, and I'm too afraid to lose Sam. The longest conversations we ever have are to put me down. She has threatened to kill herself on multiple occasions. I'm pretty sure she wants to kill me. And if she knew I was taking you to get a drink, even in an innocent way, she would stab you in the face with an ice pick because despite the fact that she is terrible to me, she is jealous beyond any measure known to man.*

"She's nice. She stays at home with Sam. She has been going to school off and on trying to become a teacher," Gary eventually recited. A familiar recital. His "image." His absent stare and monotone voice during the recital made it less believable every time.

"Um, tell me about . . ." Gary was still caught in the midst of his thoughts.

"Joey?" Katelyn asked without further prompt. "He's . . . well, he's a farmer. He works a lot. And I mean *a lot*. I wish I got more time with him. He is amazing, but it is hard because I have to think about what is best for Brandon. And Joey is fantastic with him. I just wish he didn't have to go out of town so much."

"Out of town to farm?" Gary asked. He wasn't well versed with the habits of farmers. Having grown up in Portland, he knew very little outside of what he had learned during his work.

"He does cowboy work. During the summer, he sets up for rodeos. He is in Pendleton all week, working with the bulls."

"Sounds dangerous."

Katelyn shrugged. "It takes a while to know how to work the bulls. But once you have worked with them for a while, you know how to keep yourself out of danger."

They turned the corner toward Whiskey's. Katelyn looked up and pointed out a sign: Karaoke Night. She smiled back at Gary.

"Oh no. No, no, no, no, no, no. Uh-uh, no way," Gary shook his head.

Katelyn had the biggest grin that Gary had ever seen on her. For the first time, he truly saw her happy. She was a beautiful sight to behold. Stunning. Spectacular. Breathtaking. This was looking more and more like a bad idea. She swayed back and forth, holding her hands behind her back. "Are you telling me that super calm, collect, and confident attorney man is afraid of the big stage?"

Gary chuckled. "Ugh. Look, I'll *watch* you sing. But not for me."

Katelyn crossed her arms and kept looking at him, saying nothing.

"Ask me after a couple of beers." Gary smiled.

"Deal." Katelyn opened the door, leading him in.

"My power, my pleasure, my pain. Baby, to me you're like a growing addiction I can't deny. Won't you tell me is that healthy, baby? But did you know that when it snows, my eyes become large and the light that you shine can be seen . . . baby . . ." The bald man that was on the stage had all the confidence of an American Idol competitor with all the talent of the Cleveland Browns. Dressed in a Hawaiian shirt, seventy-five pounds overweight, and lubricated beyond any legal measure. This was a sobering reminder of why Gary didn't go out that often.

Katelyn stared up at the stage. "Now *he* is a confident person."

"I think you mean lit-up person. Um, let's get a drink." Gary led them over to the bar.

"I'll take a Corona . . . and . . ?" Gary looked at Katelyn.

"Scotch on the rocks." Katelyn shouted boldly over the music. Gary looked at her with amazement. "Remember, I'm a country girl. There isn't a lot to do here when you're young outside of have children and build a liquor tolerance." Katelyn led them over a table. Gary chuckled, not sure if that was funny or a little sad about this town.

They sat and watched a few performers. Most of them they laughed at and critiqued. Most of the performers went all out to the normal songs on a karaoke night: "Don't Stop Believing," "Pour Some Sugar on Me," "Livin' on a Prayer" . . . It was a trend of catchy songs that most people either knew the lyrics to or where too liquored enough to care and attempted to sing anyways.

"So I guess it is getting close to our turn?" Katelyn asked.

Gary sighed, "Okay." He was on his second beer, and this was a lot of fun. He hadn't had a friend in a while. "Okay, okay. So you get to go first." Gary smiled.

Katelyn looked at him and pondered. "Okay then, I'll go first, but after I'm done, you're next?"

"Okay, good."

They went up to the stage and signed up for songs. Katelyn chose hers quickly. She looked through the book and found a song that Gary didn't know and said, "Oh, this is perfect."

"No, no, no . . ." Gary looked more. "Besides, you get one shot at this. You need to make it count. You aren't getting me up there again. This one!"

"How is it that you go from no confidence to Michael fucking Jackson after less than a beer?"

They walked back to the table. "This is my second beer. Thank you very much." Gary threw his head back in mock disgust.

"No, you see, it doesn't count when you get a second beer because it took you so long to finish the first one that it got warm and the owner comes by and comps you a new beer because you do work for him." She smirked.

"Okay, okay, so I'm not a drinker. You know something about me, tell me something about you."

"I am a drinker, your turn." She smiled back at him.

"Okay, hmm," Gary thought, "it's hard, ask me something."

"Okay, okay, why did you lie earlier?" she stated. She wasn't asking if he had lied. She was telling him.

"Huh?"

"Your wife. Look, I'm not a fucking idiot. I'm just a client. Well, I guess now we can upgrade the label to friend. But you are at the bar with me even though you could be with her." Who was the attorney here again?

Gary sighed. "Look, it's complicated."

"I got time." Katelyn crossed her arms and smirked back him.

He considered her for a moment. Her long brunette hair framed her face perfectly. It ran down her shoulders onto her white sweat-shirt. Her brown eyes were drawing him in more and more, and finally he decided he could trust her.

"So the truth is, we never should have gotten married." Gary stumbled through the words at first, then they just came. "I barely knew her by the time we got married. We started dating when she was a senior in high school and I was a freshman in college. I guess I thought she was someone she really wasn't. I was such a determined person. I wanted to get through school. I didn't pay attention to who she was, I paid attention to the fact that I had a girlfriend."

"You were surprised you had a girlfriend?" Katelyn said, smiling with a look of bemusement.

"Quite frankly, it was fucking weird. I had a few girlfriends in high school, but never anything serious. Actually, I would say nobody that really ever liked me in the same way. Staci did, and for some reason, that was enough for me. I never really had good luck with women, and here was one at least willing to give me the time of day."

"So how do you spend so many years with someone and not really know them?" Katelyn inquired.

"Well, I worked multiple jobs to build up my résumé and took full class loads. It was nuts. At one point, we decided that when I was done with my four years of college and got a bachelor degree we would get married. It was about it being time more than anything else. Then I went to law school a month after we were married. I studied, studied some more, and then, well, studied."

"What did she do when you were in law school?"

"She worked part-time at the mall. We saw each other maybe five to ten hours a week. It wasn't enough to get irritated with anyone."

"Were you guys, like, you know, *together?*" Katelyn made quotation marks with her fingers in the air.

"No, not really, I chalked us not having sex to us not being around each other enough, not any other issues. Then I started my career. Shortly after, she was pregnant."

"I thought you said you guys didn't ever have sex?" Katelyn rolled her eyes.

"There is a big difference between a good and healthy sex life and having sex only on special occasions due to some stupid social obligation to do so."

"I guess that makes sense. But after you got out of school, did things get better?"

"No, not really. Sam helped, for a while at least. But only for a while. Then when I started to build up enough of a reputation and workload not to have to work seventy hours a week, I realized I woke up next to a stranger. That was probably two years ago. We didn't grow apart, we just were never together." Gary spewed out the information in a hurry. Getting everything out was the most freedom he had felt in years. He spoke about his sex life without really meaning to and at first felt like he had crossed a line and said too much. But the look on Katelyn's face wasn't that he crossed a line. Gary felt like she genuinely cared.

"So why not try to get to know her? Why just lie down and be miserable?"

Gary smiled for the first time during the story. "Try? You have no idea. Date nights, movie nights, vacations, all the time and money I could muster for about a year. I don't think either of us failed in it, it's more like, it wasn't possible. Like trying to mix oil and water. It doesn't matter how hard you stir, they never stay together. Eventually, I realized that she was giving up." Gary went silent.

"So you are keeping it together for Sam?" Katelyn asked.

"The best I can, but it isn't easy. Every day I tell myself that Sam needs her, that he is what keeps her alive, and that they depend on each other. But the more I see, the harder it is to believe that. She is . . ." Gary searched for the words. "Self-destructive. She doesn't have any motivation. She doesn't care to do better. Worst of all, she doesn't about know what I care about. A good school for our son? A good neighborhood? A college fund? Those are abstract things to her. They can't be goals to her. They are just things you talk about, not things you actually put any effort toward. In reality, she is a child in a lot of ways herself. She never makes her own phone calls for doctor's appointments. She never goes shopping by herself. She couldn't hold a job when she was trying to, and she couldn't keep up with little things in life. I thought I had someone that was going to go on the journey with me, actively, not just along for the ride. After we kind of both came to that realization, things just escalated. I got yelled at more. Her needs got neglected more. It just got worse and worse."

"Sounds like she isn't healthy. Have you tried mental health help?" Katelyn asked with a great amount of care in her voice.

"We've tried everything. The only thing she can seem to stay on is pot. I know it isn't right to leave someone when they are mentally ill. You are supposed to help them. You are supposed to take the burden and bear it like a cross, not run from it. But the truth is that every day it is like a little bit of her crazy leaves her and leaks into me. Like every day I try to keep her healthy is killing me. Slowly, agonizingly, and torturously. Every aspect of my life outside of my home is under my control, and none of it at home is." Gary swallowed the last bit of the third beer that had been brought to him. They were going down fast now. He decided he needed to reverse the roles back to normal.

"I guess turnabout is fair play. Why did you lie to me?" Gary asked her.

"Unlike you," she stared at him, "I won't try to deny it." Katelyn took a sip of her third Scotch. "Ironically, I feel a lot like your wife. I don't have a lot of direction in life. A big part of that is Brandon. He is everything to me. I've been fighting with Paul for so long that

Brandon is all I can think about. Everything else has to wait, every-thing else I can figure out later." Katelyn got silent.

"I get it. I'm lucky . . ." Gary took another drink midsentence. "I am lucky because I got my career before Sam came along. I think . . . I mean, I know that I'd be in the same boat if I hadn't been able to get my education beforehand."

"Yes, you are lucky. But I wouldn't change it if it meant giving him up in any way."

"Look," Gary said, "tell me something about you, not the shitty fucking situation we have ourselves in."

"Ah, hmm, well . . . I *love* karaoke." Katelyn laughed. "I was in choir in high school, and I actually really enjoy singing. It kind of gives me some freedom. Like being a lawyer is your calling, singing is my calling."

"That's awesome," Gary said.

"No," Katelyn said sharply. "Your passion, law, pays and pays well. My passion, music, only gets me broken dreams, a broken bank account, and on occasion, a couple free drinks after a song."

With that, her song began to play.

Katelyn took one last drink and put the bottom of the glass to the ceiling. She got up from the table and began walking toward the stage. She turned around and winked at Gary. He found himself watching her body as she walked up to the stairs. It was enchanting as she moved her hips from left to right. Her long brunette hair almost touched her butt as it moved back and forth while she moved.

She turned and faced the crowd and slowly unzipped her white Colts hoodie. She took it off her shoulders to reveal her pink tank top. She tossed it toward Gary, who barely got it between two of his fingers.

"The twenty-second of loneliness, and we've been through so many things. I love my man with all honesty, but I know he's cheatin' on me." He knew that it didn't mean anything, but it was a really telling song if it did.

"I look him in his eyes, but all he tells me is lies to keep me near." Katelyn was looking deep into the eyes of some poor sucker, in addition to him, who was sitting close to the stage, watching the twenty-something woman move around the stage with an exotic aura about her.

"I'll never leave him down though, I might mess around. It's only 'cause I need some affection." She swayed her body back and forth and to the ground, meeting Gary's eyes.

"Oh, so I creep, yeah, yeah, just keep it on the down low, said nobody is supposed to know, so I creep yeah, 'cause he doesn't know what I do and no attention goes to show, oh, so I creep."

After the song, he watched her move toward the table. Maybe it was the beer. Maybe it was the atmosphere. Maybe he was just so fucking lonely. But . . . it was impossible to look away from her. The idea was a train wreck waiting to happen. But nothing else could enter his mind.

No sooner had she gotten to the table before his music started playing. Gary wandered up to the stage in the haze of his buzz and sang a terrible rendition of "Billie Jean."

"Oh my god, that was awful." Katelyn looked like she would burst into tears of laughter.

"Yes, it was," Gary agreed. "You asked, I delivered." Gary bowed to Katelyn.

"So let's do one together." Katelyn grinned.

"Oh no, no fucking way." Gary shook his head, but he knew that he would do it for her.

They walked up to the stage again. Katelyn picked out a song; Gary nodded. He hadn't even heard it before. They walked back to the table and finished the last bit of their drinks. Katelyn kept looking over at him, and she never took the smile off her face.

CHAPTER 6

● ● ● ● ● ● ●

Ask Me if I Care

O ver the next few days, the reckless night played over and over
again in Gary's mind. Well, in truth, it wasn't the actual events
of the night that played over and over again but the lustful and savage
thoughts of what might have been. After the final song, they met the
chilly air outside, and it seemed to sober them back up into reality.
It took them back to the fact that they had gone out to get a couple
drinks as friends, nothing more. The taboo nature of their encounter
made it somehow more thrilling.

During his entire relationship with Staci, he had been faithful. Never had he entertained the notion of being with another
woman. At least no more than the minimum a man could help. He
had avoided being unfaithful in an unhappy relationship because he
never put himself in a position where he could be unfaithful. No
matter how much disdain he had for Staci, he knew that he couldn't
bring himself to that point.

They had walked back to his office under the streetlights. Gary
had checked his phone over and over again for the time, realizing
Staci would be back home at any moment. Excuses played through
his mind. He decided on the way home he would pick up food and
complain about long lines if necessary. As he walked back to the
office, he listened to himself with disgust. He was becoming "that
guy."

They had innocently smiled at each and waved on the way to
their respective cars. He had imagined the moonlight shining off her
long divine hair as he put his hands on her waist and pushed against

her bewitching lips with his own. He imagined holding Katelyn's hand while walking back to the bar. He imagined the smooth touch of her pearl skin in between his fingers. He imagined her unzipping that white sweatshirt, like she had on stage, on a stage meant only for him. He imagined running his fingers through her hair while he kissed her neck and . . .

Right there. That was what he couldn't let himself imagine. The theater in his head plagued him. It tortured him with her contorted body wrapped around his. He could not have that image in his head. What upset him was that this was completely out of line with the ethical standards he had set for himself. The problem was he knew that if he acted on the feelings that he could be disbarred. He knew it could end his marriage, although that train was unlikely to stop regardless of what happened with Katelyn. The problem was that he felt like the pull he had toward her was greater than those things. That his whole life, he had been working toward being an attorney, being a senator, being a . . . somebody. Now he would throw that all away for a woman. It was fucking ridiculous.

Sam was always his saving grace. Gary's thoughts traveled to him, and it was what stopped him over the next few days from trying to pursue something more. He thought of the difference in Sam's life. With his career, Gary could pay for college tuition, a car right at sixteen, anything Sam needed or desired. He hated to think about the difference in his life if he ended up teaching political science to high school asshole teenagers who probably think that the Great Depression is something that can be controlled with Xanax, that Abraham Lincoln really was a vampire hunter, or that you can't possibly take a shit without a fucking smartphone.

The thoughts of Sam shook him back into reality.

Today Gary was sitting on a bench in court, waiting for his client's name to be called. A pretrial suppression hearing to determine if the evidence provided by the state could be admitted at trial. Gary had high hopes that he could keep some phone recordings off the record. They were recorded conversations from a wiretap. Gary had hoped that the fact that there was more than one Eddie in the thousands of phone calls grabbed by the state police would allow him to count the phone calls as hearsay as the person speaking could not be properly identified. Under Oregon law, a party to the proceeding could have their own conversations used against them. However, if the State could not show that the conversations were in fact Eddie Gutierrez, well then, the State would be unable to prove that the conversations fell within the exception, and the evidence would be held out.

This was truly the only evidence against his client. He was guilty, of course, and the thought of a man guilty of much worse than racketeering getting off without a scratch made the pit of his stomach ache. But it was his job to defend the rights, not the person. And quite frankly, the idea of screwing this up made him more fearful than Eddie Gutierrez roaming the streets.

Veronica Sanders stood with her smug look, arguing to Judge Oswald about a codefendant in the racketeering case. Her style was very straightforward. No smoke and mirrors. Gary knew that in arguments he had the upper hand, being more familiar with Judge Oswald. But Gary had doubts about what may happen if the matter went to trial. Juries rarely cared for defense lawyers. Veronica was middle-aged, with a face sort of like a pug but a beautiful figure. Juries liked straight shooters even if they didn't have the best arguments. Juries didn't like to make their decisions on technicalities. They wanted honesty. She could give them that; he couldn't. As he always did prior to a jury trial, he made note of the jurors he would want. Small-minded men who might be intimidated by a powerful woman would be ideal with her as his adversary.

"Eddie Gutierrez," Judge Oswald called, not looking up as she did so. She appeared to be in a poor mood. Eddie wasn't sure yet if this would be helpful or not to his case, but the fact that he knew it from working with her, and Ms. Sanders did not, gave him an advantage on the approach.

"Good morning, Your Honor, Gary Tornow, Oregon State Bar Number 082841, on behalf of the defendant. We are here today on a motion to suppress filed by the defense. We have learned through reviewing the police reports and extensive discovery provided in this enormous multi-defendant case that the only evidence that the

State has against Mr. Gutierrez is that they claim to have a series of recorded phone calls from a wiretap in which Mr. Gutierrez allegedly makes references to the sale of firearms and narcotics, not directly but by a code allegedly determined to be the operative coding of a racketeering group in the Greater Basin Area. For example, the code says that horses are guns, sheep is meth, etc. So, Your Honor, we are here because—"

Gary was cut off midsentence by Judge Oswald. "If they have Ms. Gutierrez's voice on these phone calls, I am certainly going to let them in. You are, of course, well-rehearsed in the exception to the hearsay rule, which allows evidence of out-of-court statements made by parties to the action, especially if those statements satisfy elements of the claim."

Veronica Sanders turned a smug look toward Gary. But Gary's confidence went through the roof. She had missed the boat, again, because Judge Oswald was going down the exact path he wanted her to. "Yes, Your Honor, I understand that. However, that is why we are here. The person who introduces the hearsay evidence has the burden of proving that it lies within the exception. Here, the State cannot do that because they are unable to verify that it is Mr. Gutierrez on the phone." Gary paused for effect and then continued on.

"There are 424 hours of phone conversations. The State has narrowed down Mr. Gutierrez's phone calls to approximately one hour and thirty minutes of time. However, there are three men indicted in this racketeering case out of twenty-five that have the name Eddie. Further, four codefendants have the last name Gutierrez." Again, he paused, enjoying how Veronica's face melted from beautiful to bitter in the blink of an eye.

Gary pushed forward. "The State has claimed that everyone in the operation used burner phones, month-to-month phones that are cheap and can be disposed of routinely, and so the phone numbers are irrelevant. I listened to all the conversations involving other Eddies and other Gutierrezes. It took roughly twenty-eight hours of time. Here is the problem. Although most of it is in Spanish, the content isn't the issue. The issue is that the voice labeled as 'Eddie Gutierrez'"—he made the quotation signs with his fingers—"that is the conversations that the State has labeled as his conversations, is heard in roughly five hours of phone calls labeled under other code-fendants' phone calls." Gary paused again to let this sink in.

"Okay, so if I understand," Judge Oswald said slowly, "you're saying that they cannot prove that those conversations were in fact his because they labeled other phone calls wrong and they can't differentiate the voices, meaning that they failed to meet the burden of proof for the exception." It wasn't a question, it was a succinct legal argument made in his favor by the very judge deciding his client's fate. She looked at Ms. Sanders. "Thoughts?"

Ms. Sanders stood open jaw for a moment, stuttered slightly, then began, "Well, ah, Your Honor, we have the officers subpoenaed here today that listened to the recordings. They can testify that they believe that these conversations are with Eddie Gutierrez based upon the timing of them. Although the only tangible evidence we have is the phone calls, we do know when Mr. Gutierrez was on and off the farm that many of the members used as an operating base. And—"

"What did you find at the operating base?" The judge cut her off.

"Unfortunately, the warrants did not find anything illegal," Sanders began. "It was where we found writings that helped us crack codes used by the racketeering operation. However, it seems that this was either only a meeting place, or they had been tipped off prior to our search." Sanders stopped, not to pause for dramatic effect but because she had nothing else, and she knew it.

The judge let the silence set in, considering the matter for the moment. "Here is what I am going to do. I'm going to hold the decision for fifteen days. At that time, I want affidavits from the State narrowing down specifically why they believe these calls are connected to Eddie Gutierrez. If they cannot produce them with more evidence than the timing was simply right, I'll go ahead and grant the motion. I suppose at that point Mr. Tornow will be asking for a dismissal?" The judge looked toward Gary.

"Yes, Your Honor. Effectively all the evidence that could be used against Mr. Gutierrez of any substance would not be admissible," Gary stated.

"And I'll grant the motion to dismiss at that point unless the State produces anything else. Is there anything else for this defendant?" the judge questioned them while staring back down at paperwork.

"No, Your Honor," Gary and Veronica chanted in unison.

Gary shook his client's hand on the way out of the courtroom, still thoroughly distracted as he had been for days.

He looked down at his phone to check for his next appointment. He had a meeting with Robert Murray, the new client he had met in the jail a couple weeks ago. Out on bail, Robert had been allowed to return to work; but as a local businessman, he had to manage his business from home and watch his profits plummet. It didn't bode well for Gary, who knew that with his business going down that Robert was unlikely to be able to afford additional fees after what he had already paid. Gary sighed on his way back to his office. The walk seemed to take longer than it had in the past. He used to fill his spare time with thoughts about his son, thoughts about work, thoughts about the Blazers. And now . . . it was filled with things that made his stomach churn, but his heart burn with passion.

He opened the door and walked past the receptionist's desk. Marti had put a sign on the front door that the office was temporarily closed, apparently on an errand. He checked his e-mails absentmindedly and answered them until he heard the gentle knock on the front door.

"Hi, Robert, how are you doing?" Gary opened the door.

Robert walked in with a force smile on his face, "Good afternoon, Mr. Tornow."

"Come on in, Robert." They made their way back to the office, Gary flipping through various documents in his hand as they walked. "Have a seat."

Robert sat. The look on his face was scared. This man was craven. Fearful that his long line of sins had finally caught up to him at this juncture in his life, and for something that could be construed as innocent . . .

"Robert, tell me what has happened since we last spoke. Last time we spoke, if I recall, was the day your mom bailed you out. Is that correct?" Robert nodded. Gary reached for the file. "So I've spoken to the district attorney's office. There is good news and, of course, bad news. The good news is that it appears this is a case we could try to have a reasonably good chance of winning. The bad news is that the district attorney has a high belief that you are guilty of these crimes. Apparently, your wife has told her daughter several things about your past that concerns her. Are you and your wife still together?"

Robert nodded. "She is sleeping in the guest room right now. She had left, but came back home a few days ago and said that she would try to understand why . . . why . . . Well, she said that she knows she made a commitment in front of God and that if I am willing to . . ." Robert paused, his breathing became much heavier.

"Confess?" Gary guessed.

"In a way. She wants me to apologize. She wants me to seek help. She wants me to confess my sins to God. She said that she needed to know if something happened in the past. But I told her nothing has happened, but she doesn't believe me." Robert stopped, but Gary didn't say anything. He wanted Robert to carry on but when he was ready to begin, not forced to do so. Gary needed to know what he was up against, and he needed Robert to tell him his history. It was likely irrelevant to the current case and likely that the statute of limitations was still in play, meaning he couldn't be prosecuted if something had happened in the past.

Robert didn't take the silent invitation, so Gary prodded. "The prosecutor seems to think that you do in fact have a past. So I'm not trying to judge what has happened in the past. I'm going to do that to you. My job is to combat the current charges. I need to know what possibly could be there that we need to be concerned about. Your wife can't testify at trial about what you have talked about with her. She can answer basic questions about your past. The evidence is unlikely to even be allowed in, but *the alleged past incidents are fueling this prosecutors fire."* Gary emphasized the final words and allowed Robert to soak in them.

"About a year ago," Robert began, "well, I guess it starts further back than that. My brother is in prison, attempted murder of his wife. Nobody would have believed him capable. In fact, I still have a hard time believing it. We lost complete contact with the rest of his part of the family after that. None of kids ever called again, either myself or my parents. Don's wife just cut us out." Robert paused, and Gary could tell that the fact that these kids had been cut off from him caused him an immense amount of pain.

Gary began to feel his heart beat faster and his breathing get faster. He could not understand why. He felt balls of sweat form on his hands; he felt his stomach twist, but his mind had not yet caught up with his physical reaction. Why? What was it that this meant to Gary? Emotion during cases wasn't his thing, but this was likely due to recent personal emotional issues. Perhaps Gary's issues in life were simply catching up with him. Perhaps the stone-cold persona that he had taken on for all these years had been pierced.

"I'm still not getting, what exactly—" Gary stopped midsentence, allowing Robert the opportunity to carry on.

"Well, again, it must have been about a year ago. I saw my brother for the first time. My wife and I both went. I had talked to him a few times, but . . ." Robert paused and thought about his words for a moment. "Seeing your brother in prison, no matter what kind of person he is, well . . . that is hard. It took a lot out of me. Talking on the phone is one thing, but this was harder than that. Anyways, he showed us the letters that he kept receiving. Quite frankly, Jerry is nuts. She just can't keep her mouth shut and has to say something, whether it is the truth or a lie. He can't write her back, you see, because she is the victim in the crime. But apparently, she can write all she wants, and no one seems to care what it is." Robert paused again, and Gary gathered he would finally figure out where the track Robert was laying led to.

Robert pushed forward, practically choking over the words, "Most of the letters were accusations about Donald touching his kids. Well, she called them her kids. She had two girls coming into the relationship. But Donald had raised them. He denied it. Then . . ." Robert slowed down and looked completely away from Gary "Then . . . she wrote a letter saying that she thought I'd touched the girls." Robert finished, barely audible by the end as the volume of his voice went down.

"If," Gary inquired, "they are asked, your nieces I mean, what are they going to say?"

"I don't know," Robert said, staring blankly at the wall behind Gary. Gary didn't need to know more. He already knew that Robert had touched the girls as well. The way he stated the accusation was enough.

"Okay, we will work around that issue if it comes up," Gary said. Robert filed through the police report. He pointed out the issues of inconsistency within the report. It took about a half hour to get through all of it.

Then Gary noticed something that he overlooked before. It was such a common nickname for Robert he hadn't bothered asking and quite frankly wasn't sure why he inquired now. "Do you go by Bob?" Gary asked.

"Just for the kids, usually," Robert stated. "When I became an adult, I started going by Robert, but most kids still call me Bob. Easier to remember and more fun." This time, and for the first time, a real smile crossed Robert's face.

Gary finished going through the discovery, wroth with issues, and then quietly escorted Robert out of the office.

Gary could not shake the feeling he had, as though he had had an epiphany without having actual realization. Gary absentmindedly checked his e-mail, preparing to leave the office. Then he saw a settlement offer come into his e-mail from Adam Rose, another attorney in town. Adam represented Paul Bettles, Katelyn Gail's baby daddy.

Then it dawned on him. He rushed over to the file cabinet and violently opened his cabinet. He pulled out Katelyn's file and opened it up on the desk. He stood, rather than sat, anxious to see if his realizations were true. He looked at the notes he took from their last interview. It hadn't been a huge issue to remember the details at the time, but he remembered he scribbled something down . . .

Then he found the things he was looking for. In the corner of his notes was written: "Stepdad, Donald, prison, mom victim of assault, client w/ sex abuse issues in past, blackouts."

Gary always wrote the down the names of important people in his cases on the first page, and he rifled back. Katelyn's mom was named Jerry.

Then Gary heard the words of Katelyn ring from before their adventure to the bar together. He heard the words that made him realize that Katelyn needed a friend. And he heard "But I have dreams about my Uncle Bob touching me" ring out in his head loudly in Katelyn's angelic voice.

CHAPTER 7

S'getti

He didn't need to know. He didn't need to *know*. But for some fucking reason, the things in his mind that simultaneously made him a borderline genius of an attorney and halfway crazy forced him to know. He might not have put it together had he not looked at her file. *Why did he look? Why did he need to care?*

Gary paced around his office. It was nearly 6:00 p.m. Robert had left nearly an hour ago. Gary had been trying to calm down before leaving. He risked the anger of Staci if he left too much later, but he wasn't sure if he could hold himself together tonight, this night of all nights. The images he had hours before of his body contorted with Katelyn's, her engulfing his manhood in her mouth, making her scream in pleasure . . . they were replaced by new images, more dangerous ones. He wanted to hold her. Tell her it would be okay. Tell her that he would do something about it.

Gary thought before that lusting for her was dangerous. It wasn't. Lust was . . . lust was easy. You could take care of lust by yourself in the shower. But this kind of care, this kind of need to comfort . . . *that* was dangerous. What was more, he now had the images of Robert Murray's body lying limp on the ground in a pool of blood, being left for vultures in the Mojave Desert, and Robert's penis severed from his body for his sins with a serrated blade. They were images he could not afford. Not when he was responsible for defending the man's rights.

Gary began to breathe a little easier. Perspective. He wasn't defending him against crimes committed against Katelyn. He was defending his rights for crimes committed against a faceless child. It didn't make it better as it always had before. It allowed Gary to slip back into his emotionless persona that he was usually able to find solace in for only a moment. After the temporary calm, he realized another painful reality that again set his insides on fire. He was sworn to secrecy by the rules of his profession. Never could he tell Katelyn. He couldn't hint at it. He couldn't tell her to explore the issues more. Nothing. He could not break confidentiality. He could not risk everything over that, as he already thought he was with the thoughts of Katelyn and him.

Gary did not know what direction life was heading in. But he knew this: he wanted Katelyn to be a part of it, even just as a friend, a client, a person to wave hi to in the store. If years down the road, something else, fine. But he knew that it would be impossible. It would be impossible because he would know the identity of the person who hurt her. She knew, but her memories were fuzzy. He heard the words from the perpetrator, the abuser. No meaningful relationship at any level could survive with such an omission.

Gary had finally calmed all the way down. Logic had set in. "If I can't tell her and that would mean we couldn't have anything meaningful, then any slight amount of risk that this causes isn't worth it. I have to stay away from her outside of the office," he thought out loud. It strengthened his resolve. And although the lustful thoughts remained, somehow the realizations of the night made it easier to press forward in spite of them, knowing that if lust was the only thing he had to combat that he could do so with ease.

Gary walked out of the office, closed the door, and locked it for the night before, making his way to his car. Driving home felt as it ever did. With a heavy heart, he pulled onto his street. He expected his usual greeting. Staci's blue sedan would be in the driveway, as she never went anywhere except one night a week to a friend's house, and when he came inside, she would depart for another room, leaving him with Sam.

Gary was surprised to see that as he pulled up, the lights in the house were on and the car was nowhere to be found. Gary was not use to anything outside of the usual "routine." He walked up to the house and checked the door. It was locked.

He grabbed the keys out of his pocket and noticed that it sounded like the TV was on. That wasn't surprising. When Staci did leave, she rarely remembered to turn things off.

Gary pushed open the door. Gary had not looked up as he made his way toward the bedroom.

"Daddy!" he heard Sam's voice call out from near the TV.

Gary looked at him in shock. Her car wasn't here, and Sam was? Where was she at? Was she somewhere in the house? Had they been out earlier and they had to walk home because of an issue with the car? It seemed unlikely. "Sam, how are you doing, little buddy?" Gary stated, trying to not act too alarmed.

"Good, I'm watching nigh' nigh' show," Sam said in a matter-of-fact manner, looking back at the TV.

Indeed he was. He was watching what always seemed to be on at about this time. This channel seemed to be catering to those in the eastern time zone as lullabies played on the west coast at only 6:00 p.m. "Where is Mommy at, Sam?" Gary asked.

Sam shrugged his shoulders. "I'm hungry, Daddy." He looked up at him with his large round eyes.

"Okay, buddy, let me go check on Mommy real quick." Had she told him she was leaving? Had she sneaked out of the basement? Had she even realized Sam was with her before she left?

Gary left Sam in the living room and went room by room to try to find Staci. He checked upstairs first, looking back at Sam as he exited each room to check on him. Gary was concerned about the nonchalant manner in which Sam had answered about his mom not being home. Did she do this often and Gary just didn't know?

Lastly, Gary checked the basement. When he opened the door, the lights downstairs where on. Faint music was playing. The basement door to the outside was shut but was unlocked. He opened the spare room. The smell of marijuana overwhelmed him at first, then it began to clear. The music was coming from her mp3 player lying on the floor. Staci was nowhere to be found.

Gary walked back up to the living room, sat on the tan couch, and buried his hands in his face. He didn't know what he could do. Could he carry on living like this when Sam was constantly in danger?

"Daddy?" Sam walked up to him.

"Oh, buddy, I'm sorry, I forgot you were hungry. What do you want?"

Sam stood there for a moment, swaying back and forth and smiling at his father. "Um . . . S'getti." Sam tilted his head to the side as he said it.

Gary really didn't need to ask; it was his favorite meal. "Okay, what kind of sauce, red or white?"

"Red." Sam nodded with certainty.

Gary took him by the hand, and they walked into the kitchen. Gary worked his way through the cupboards. "Sam, it doesn't look we have noodles, buddy. Do you want anything else?"

"I want s'getti. Can we buy it, Daddy?"

Gary smiled back at him. "Sure, buddy." He looked Sam over. It appeared that he hadn't had a bath all day, and he was wearing clothes slightly too small for him. Gary drew a bath and left Sam to play with his boat as he went into his room, looking for clothes. The drawers were bare. There were barely any clothes clean. He eventually found a shirt and some jeans that smelled as if they hadn't been worn even though they looked pretty wrinkled on the floor. Gary noted that he would need to add doing Sam's laundry to the list of chores he needed to double-check on daily because Staci simply wouldn't get to them.

He checked on Sam every minute or so as he changed from his suit into plain jeans, T-shirt, sneakers, and hoodie. He dried Sam off and dressed him quickly. Gary took the time to shut off everything in the house, as he always did, hoping beyond hope that Staci would eventually take the hint that they paid too much for electricity and that everything didn't need to be on when no one was there.

They got into the car, and Gary strapped Sam into the car seat. On the way to the store, Sam talked Gary's ears off about his favorite toy, his light saber that they had gotten from the circus several months before. Sam had always used it in their fake sword fights.

They pulled into the parking lot, and Sam immediately pointed out a shopping cart in the return area that had a front resembling a race car. They got out of the car and made their way toward the chosen shopping cart. While rummaging through the cupboards and finding little in the way of edible food, he had made a mental shopping list.

Before they began looking for groceries, they did their customary trip to the video game section and looked at all the newer games. Sam wasn't quite old enough to enjoy them with Gary yet, but Sam loved to watch them. He loved to sit with Gary as he explained everything to him, often holding an unconnected controller in his hands while his father played.

They made their way around to the toys shortly thereafter. As usual, Gary told Sam he could pick out something small, and like usual, Sam picked up some blowing bubbles and Play-Doh.

"Daddy, I want f'uit snack," Sam blurted out as they had finally made their way to the groceries.

"Okay, let's get some," Gary said as he diverted from the items he needed to make sure Sam got some. Sam's *R*s and *P*s were the hardest for him.

Sam pointed to the box he wanted once they reached the aisle, the one with Mario on the front. "Any other special requests?" Gary asked.

Sam seemed to think for a moment and then shook his head no. "I'm hungry." Gary opened the box of fruit snacks in the store and opened one for Sam.

"We still have a little shopping to do, buddy. Let's get through a couple more aisles." Gary smiled at Sam and messed up his hair.

They walked down a few more aisles, grabbing juice, cookies, soup, etc. Then they made their way to the spaghetti aisle. Gary grabbed a few jars of sauce and placed them in the cart. He then grabbed a box of spaghetti noodles and a box of macaroni shells. "Which one?" He turned around and showed Sam.

Sam pointed at the box of macaroni. Gary thought it over and decided to throw both in the cart in case Sam changed his mind later.

They made their way to the checkout and picked the shortest line possible. Sam pointed at some candy, and Gary reached over and grabbed it and placed it in the cart. A familiar yet at the same time foreign intoxicating aroma enchanted Gary. It was as if his body had sensed the smell before he actually processed it, as his heart had begun to beat faster and his palms became sweaty before the realization hit him.

"Hi, stranger," he heard in her giggly voice from behind him.

Gary looked back and saw Katelyn dressed in the same white Colts hoodie, jeans, and boots she had the other night. Then he looked at the basket, the same as his, a racecar in the front. This must be Brandon.

"Good to see you. Is this Brandon?" Gary smiled at her, trying not to smile to hard.

"Ya, I'm Brandon, I'm three," the frail-looking child spurted out before his mother. "Mommy, there is a boy with him. Can we play?"

This was a very smart and very forward child. He had brown hair and eyes like Katelyn, but his ears and nose were overlarge and looked nothing like the traits of Katelyn's family.

"Bug, I don't know. They probably have plans." Katelyn smiled back at Gary. Gary wondered if they had had the same thoughts. That perhaps she knew they needed to keep away from each other.

"Ya, Sam and I are going to go home and eat spaghetti," Gary said, looking at Brandon.

"Is your name Sam?" yelled Brandon over Gary's words.

Sam was looking back and replied with a nod. The two children couldn't be more opposites. Sam was smart, intuitive, but an introvert in many ways already at the age of three.

"Mommy, Sam is going to come play with us, K?" Brandon spurted out.

Wow, just wow. That was all Gary could say over and over again in his mind. "Sounds like we have to make a play date, huh?" Gary gave in with the idea that he could dodge actually meeting her later if needed.

"I don't think we have much of a say in it." Katelyn chuckled and smiled.

"Daddy, I want to play now," Gary had hoped that the look of shock hadn't shown on his face. Sam rarely spoke in front of him and Staci in such a bold manner. Here he was speaking in front of Katelyn and Brandon like it was nothing.

"Son, I don't know what they are doing tonight, buddy." Gary didn't look up, hoping Katelyn would back him up somehow.

"Well, we are going to jump over to Chuckles after this to play during dinner. You guys are welcome to come along. You won't be charging me your hourly rate, will you?" she joked with Gary.

Gary looked down at the items in his basket. Nothing that looked like it was going to spoil. He was out of excuses and gave into the smiles of his son. Fast food served by a psychotic clown and playing in a baby-feces-infested ball pit wasn't exactly his idea of a square meal, but he was out of arguments. "Ya, we'll meet you up there."

CHAPTER 8

• • • • • • ●

I Killed Your Cat, You Druggy Bitch

Gary and Sam had gotten out of the store and arrived at the restaurant first. As billed, there was a giant play structure with multiple slides, tunnels, and a ball pit. They waited in the lobby for Katelyn and Brandon to arrive. He watched her red car drive up to the restaurant as dusk set in.

"Hey, so we don't eat here that often. What do you suggest?" Gary asked Katelyn.

"Well, Brandon likes the chicken nuggets. I usually get a salad," Katelyn suggested.

"Okay, it's my treat then," Gary added.

"You really don't need to . . ." Katelyn started.

"Trust me, I do," Gary interrupted. "I charge you more money than I can afford to pay myself. I think I can spare the fifteen bucks."

Katelyn smiled at him. "Couldn't afford yourself? I find that hard to believe."

"Well, maybe I could afford myself. But I would sure hate paying for me. What kind of salad do you get here?"

"It is like a Western salsa salad. Has corn and stuff in it. It's okay. I mostly come here because Brandon likes it." She turned back to look at the two boys, who were sitting behind them on spinning chairs and twisting them back and forth.

Gary moved forward in the line and ordered the meal, thinking about what he was doing to his son. He tried to avoid fast food when he could. Basically, the ingredients of these "chicken" nuggets were processed raccoon rib meat, water, salt, lips, dicks, and assholes. He got Katelyn's salsa salad and ordered a Caesar salad for himself.

They sat down next to the play structure, and the boys ran off, neglecting the meals that began to grow cold. Well, colder than they had been when they first got them. They looked like they had been sitting idle for some time. Gary called Sam back for a moment, realizing he probably hadn't eaten all day, and he compromised by grabbing a chicken nugget and running off.

"So you put up with all the bullshit from your wife because of him?" Katelyn asked rhetorically. "It is amazing what we will put up for them."

Both Katelyn and Gary gazed at the play structure for a few moments, watching the kids play together. They chased each other around in circles. It looked like they could be at it for hours.

"I'd do anything for him," Gary broke the silence, but his eyes remained fixated on the children. Partially because he was talking about Sam, partially because he didn't want to get lost in her eyes. "Life's complicated. It's like I had this script I was supposed to follow." Gary paused and tried to pace his breathing, having begun to breathe at a quickened pace. "Then all of a sudden, it felt like I kept trying to read the script while everyone was doing improv. Even the simplest things began to not make sense."

"God, smart people are fucking complicated." Katelyn laughed. "Look, I had a drinking buddy, kind of a boyfriend, but more of a fuck buddy. The condom broke. Simple. No script, just faulty latex."

Katelyn paused and looked at her salad. "So this script," Katelyn began to ask, "didn't you ever just like, ya know, live?" Katelyn asked.

Gary pondered for a second and smiled dimly. "Sometimes. But I was always told that if you work your ass off from the age of eighteen to twenty-five, then you could play the rest of your life, and that if you played from eighteen to twenty-five, you worked hard the rest of your life. I was always so driven, I just missed a lot."

"Wait, wait. So in high school, you never . . ." Katelyn began.

Gary stopped her abruptly by shaking his head vigorously. "Unless it involved dungeons, dragons, or math, then no. I basically stumbled my way through high school, at least socially. I didn't even kiss a girl until halfway into my junior year. As for parties, my friends knew how to eat junk food and pound soda, but not beer. And after that, I concentrated too much on the future. I went to the bar a couple times after the end of term, but never that often. So, ya, a script." Gary poked at his salad a bit, mostly because it was in front of him.

Katelyn looked at him with a sad look at first and then said, "Wait, you've got to be fist-fucking me. You never kissed a girl until you were like seventeen? I don't buy it for a second. You are outgoing enough to be an attorney. You had to at least kiss a girl, right?"

"See, you have it in reverse. I'm more outgoing *because* I'm an attorney. It gives me confidence because now I'm not just some nerd. I'm someone people respect without them having to even look at me." Gary smiled slightly. "But you have to understand. It's sort of worse than before. I grew out of being an introvert by force. But being who I am now, it doesn't make me more desirable. It doesn't give me self-esteem. Being an attorney, I get women all the time looking at me for all the wrong reasons. Not because I'm handsome or funny or nice or anything like that. I mean, I'm nice and sometimes can be funny if you like puns at least. But the truth is, people see money. It couldn't be further from the truth though. I make enough to get by, but just like everyone else, it's paycheck to paycheck."

It all got heavy really fast. Why did their conversations always go like this? Couldn't they talk about the weather, the triumphs of a local sports team, or the best kind of cheese? How could he expect that their relationship would remain only that of client and attorney or just friends when every conversation they had was a deep conversation about life?

Katelyn appeared to have the same sentiment as she asked another question. "Okay, so I don't know that much about you other than you are an attorney, are in a shitty relationship, have a fucked-up image of the world, and think it should go by script, and you have a kid. Tell me something else. Like what is your favorite color?"

"Oh, forest green, easy. You?" Gary shot back.

"Lilac. Okay, you ask a question."

"Favorite cartoon as a kid?" Gary asked.

"Um, *My Little Pony*."

"Ugh, really? Shit, I had you pegged as a tomboy."

Katelyn chuckled. "There is a big difference between a tomboy and a country girl. I like to get dirty, but in sundress and nice boots." Katelyn took a drink or her soda and nibbled at the salad that was still mostly there. The kids continued to run through the structure as they both looked over. "Okay, favorite movie?"

"Hmm. Well, like recently, or all-time?" Gary asked to clarify.

"All-time. They don't make good movies anymore," Katelyn stated in a matter-of-fact tone.

"Hands down, easiest question. *The Boondock Saints.*" Katelyn choked on her soda as Gary answered.

"Absolutely awesome. No way. I never meet *anyone* who loves that movie as much as me. Do you like the second one too?" Katelyn asked, excited.

"I love it, but not as much. It's awesome, don't get me wrong. But it isn't the Saints that are the best part. Willem Dafoe is perfect in the first one. I really wish they used him more in the second one."

"Wow, see, I love the Saints," Katelyn began.

"Oh, *come on.* Everywoman loves the saints. They are so good-looking that they give straight men second thoughts. Give me something besides the guys with nice abs," Gary interrupted.

"Fine, okay then." Katelyn laughed loudly. "Well, okay, so here is something. Every time that I am in a hurry, I always yell, 'Pack your shit, pack your shit.'"

"Oh my god, yes, that is awesome. See, I wish I just had some-thing in my back pocket as cool as the prayer they do. Ya know what I mean? But of course, I don't kill anybody, so I never have a time like that. I thought about adopting something cool, like when I begin a hearing for work. For example, I always thought about pretending to smell the dirt on the ground like they do before a battle in *Gladiator.*"

"Okay, starting to understand why you didn't get any action in high school." Katelyn was glowing as she smiled. He hated him-self for wanting to know more about her, but it was like a drug. An addiction. An impulse he couldn't resist. The intoxicating nature of her words, of her smell, of her beauty . . . It burned his insides with passion. He had worked so hard to run from her all week, and it came to this.

"Thanks." Gary rolled his eyes and finished off his soda. "And by the way, I never said I didn't get any action in high school."

"Did you?" She stared him down with a giant grin on her face.

"No, I just didn't say I hadn't." Gary began to laugh.

"Jeez, you and your fucking technicalities. God, it's exhausting. Okay, so I'll make you a deal then, Mr. Nerd." Katelyn finished her last bite of salad. "If we ever off anyone together, I'll say the stupid prayer with you. Deal?"

"Deal." Gary reached his hand over, and they shook on it.

They continued to talk for a while as the kids played. She laughed at his words in a way that most people never did. Every time she flipped her hair and he got a scent of her perfume, he could feel his body physically tremble with want. The thoughts of ravaging her interrupted his coherent thoughts during their conversation. It was barbaric of him, but it didn't matter. It felt like nothing else matter. He had never before understood desire. He had never understood want until now. The fiery burn that went through his veins was something that no other need in life had ever caused.

"Daddy, can Brandon come home with us?" A dangerous question. *Why, yes, Sam, let me take Brandon home with us and explain to your mother that we had dinner with him and his mom, my gorgeous client, who I'm having sexually explicit thoughts about.* "Um, sorry, Sam, but not tonight, buddy."

"Ya, buddy, it's getting late. Brandon and I gotta get home." Katelyn backed Gary up.

They gathered their things up and put the shoes on the boys.

"So I guess I'll see you in my office soon. We have your trial next week," Gary told Katelyn.

"Ya, I think that we have an appointment on Friday for prep or something," Katelyn said.

"Okay, I'll see you then." They walked away awkwardly, not really sure what to say to each other.

Gary buckled Sam into his car seat. He watched as Katelyn walked Brandon to her car. He watched her hips move back and forth in her jeans. She stirred his insides, even fifty feet away.

As he began to drive home, Gary looked down at his phone. Three missed calls, all from Staci. Really? After not being home with Sam when he got home, she is the one panicking? He took a deep breath and prepared himself for the worst.

CHAPTER 9

● ● ● ● ● ● ●

Chocolate Milk, Blood, and Toilet Water

Gary drove up to the house, nauseated more than he had ever had before. What was he going to say? Sam could tell her anything. Innocent or not, Staci would only see red. Gary had planned on confronting Staci on leaving Sam alone. But he knew now that those words would likely fall on deaf ears. After missing three calls, Gary could only imagine the rage she had worked herself into.

Staci's car was in the driveway, and the lights were all on in the house. He pulled into the driveway. Sam had fallen asleep on the way home. He got Sam out of his car seat and held his head against his shoulder in an effort to keep him asleep. Sam lifted his head for a moment and began to stir, but only the moment. He fell back asleep almost instantly. Gary walked up to the door and turned the knob.

The explosion was instantaneous. The fury raised the temperature like an oven.

"Were the *fuck* were you? Where did you take my son? You fucker. What the hell? I'm down in the basement for five minutes, and I come up, and he is *gone*. And you don't answer your goddamn phone. You *fuck*." The slap that went across his face unblocked. He knew better. He shielded Sam, knowing she wouldn't hit him on purpose but unsure what could happen by accident.

Staci kept yelling at Gary, with Sam in his arms. Gary sat Sam down quickly on the couch, and he woke with a start, looking around the room in fright. "You weren't home," Gary said quietly. "I looked everywhere, and your car wasn't here. And five minutes? I bathed Sam, and we searched for dinner. You weren't here. He is three. What the hell is wrong with you? You reek like pot, and you are supposed to be watching Sam. He doesn't deserve this." Another slap. This one nearly knocked Gary over, but he stood his ground. He felt liquid build around his tongue. Blood was trying to make its way out of his mouth, but he held it shut, trying not to let her see it.

He began to walk toward the hallway and absentmindedly took out his phone. "So who is she?" Staci was trembling with anger as she asked.

"You're crazy," Gary didn't even look back.

Gary sensed her move toward him, and he quickly turned. She had gotten right behind him and began to reach for his phone. He put it behind him. There was nothing to hide on there, but it was the way she did it.

"I'm your wife, and I can't look at your phone. You are a piece of shit, Gary. A piece of goddamn *shit*." She flipped him off and pushed his face with her middle finger until the back of his head hit the wall in the hallway. She grabbed at the phone, and he finally gave in.

"Fine!" She had backed off. He threw the phone at her, hitting her square in the face. He hadn't mean to; he only meant to toss it. It left a red mark but wasn't nearly hard enough to do more than stun her.

She grabbed the phone and threw it back at him. He ducked, and it hit the wall behind him. It had a hard plastic cover on it and was practically indestructible. He had bought it so Sam could play it without it getting broke. It bounced back, closer to her than him.

"Who the fuck is she? I'll fucking kill her!" Staci shouted.

He didn't know what did it, but something erupted inside him. A sudden urge to fight back. She had unlocked the phone. Gary grabbed at it, and she pulled away. She ran straight into the bath-room and tried to slam the door.

Gary got his foot in the door just in time. He felt the wood slam against his foot, but he held it there. She pushed on the door as if she was trying to separate the foot from the rest of the leg. He pushed at the door, and she flew backward onto the floor. She jumped back at him, trying to get him out of the bathroom. She pushed with all her weight against the door again, and it hit Gary in the head as he pushed in. It bounced back, and he entered nonetheless.

Staci was at the toilet and threw the phone in. She slammed the lid shut and she sat on the seat. Gary didn't go for her. He tried to lift the seat to get to the phone. He got to the floor and tried to lift her off the seat when the seat itself wouldn't move. She slapped him in the face, and the force knocked his head into the porcelain sink.

The adrenaline in his veins didn't allow him to feel the pain, so the blood that ran into his right eye came as somewhat of a shock. The look on Staci's face was one of horror. What she had done appeared to have kicked her back into reality.

Staci stood up and walked out of the bathroom. She slammed something as she left, but something smaller than the door. Gary presumed she was going to get ice or something. Every other time she had snapped, she always over compensated right afterward. He was dazed and felt lightheaded from the blood. He reached over into the toilet and grabbed out his phone. The screen had bright pink colored lines from it. It was ruined or close to it.

Gary heard the basement door slam. He stood up and grabbed ahold of the sink, trying to gain his balance. With horror, he saw Sam standing in the doorway. Sam's eyes were full of disturbance and shock. Gary looked at the mirror attached to the medicine cabinet. The cabinet hung slightly open. Gary closed it the rest of the way and looked at his image. The right side of his face was stained with blood. His dark hair was matted against his head. He pooled water in his hands and splashed it on his face in an attempt to clean the blood and then wiped what he could of the blood onto a towel next to the sink.

After the blood was clear, more began to spill. He opened the medicine cabinet and grabbed medical tape and gauze. He continued to clear the wound periodically with the towel and eventually got enough gauze to stick to subdue the cut. He put the bandaging supplies back in the cabinet. But as he closed it, he noticed that the medicine appeared to have been gone through in a hurry.

Gary quickly rifled through the medicine quickly to see if his suspicion was correct. The painkillers appeared to be there. Then he thought back in his head. The muscle relaxers for his neck . . . where were they? He double-checked. They were nowhere to be found.

Gary grabbed Sam out of the hallway and put him in the living room. He put on a TV show quickly, fumbling the remote as he did so. He kissed Sam on the head; this was going to be a long night. How long? Gary didn't know yet.

Gary got up and walked toward the basement door. He got to the basement door and paused. Why? Did he need to do anything? Was it wrong? He thought of the clear path to his freedom. Let her die, he thought. He could just let her die. Let her do it. It was simple. Do nothing, and it was all over. He thought of Katelyn and how easy this made it. How he would no longer be someone yearning to be with someone other than his wife. No divorce, no custody battle, no more pain. Then he looked up. Sam was standing in the hallway.

"I'm thirsty, Daddy. I want chocolate milk." Sam stumbled through the sentence, half asleep.

Gary grabbed the milk and a cup in haste. He then grabbed the mix and threw together the milk quickly. He handed it to Sam and guided him toward the living room.

His mother. As much pain as Staci caused Gary, as terrible of a person as she was, Gary couldn't do it to Sam. Even a screwed-up mother was better than no mother at all. The idea of having to go through life knowing your mom choked on a bottle of muscle relaxers when you were three, not even your need to have a mother or her relationship with you being enough to keep her alive. That was not what Gary wanted for Sam.

He pulled open the basement door quickly and took the stairs at a faster pace than might have been safe. He had wasted so much time fucking around with the idea in his mind that he was worried. He looked toward the finished room and saw the light on.

In case she wasn't dead on the floor, he peeked around the door first. And then he saw her. She was lying on her stomach. Her head was facing away from Gary. Then he saw the bottle on the floor. Empty. Gary ran over toward her and rolled Staci toward him. Her eyes were closed. Her breathing was heavy. Gary felt her neck for her pulse. It was there, but faint. He thought. Would he call an ambulance? With what, his phone was soaking wet on the bathroom floor. Her phone? He looked around. It was nowhere to be found. He quickly looked through her pockets. There it was; it was wrapped in a printed picture of a forest that Gary did not recognize. It was off.

He tried to turn it on. Dead, just as she would be if it didn't turn on. He looked around the walls. Her charger was plugged into the wall farthest from him. He ran toward it and plugged it in. He ran back to her and waited for the sound of the phone turning on to jingle. She had drool coming from her mouth.

His heart was hardening again, and he was regretting his decision already. Why did he have to? It was so simple. He found her too late. He didn't realize what she was doing. He looked up and saw his reflection on the old television in the corner. He saw the bandages on his face. He thought about the blood likely sitting splattered on the sink and on the bathroom floor. What kind of questions would be asked? Was there any way to construe this to make it look like he had . . . ?

He didn't have to say the rest of the question in his head. The jingle from the phone turning itself on came on at that moment. He jumped up and ran toward the phone.

CHAPTER 10

A Madwoman Sees What She Sees

The walls of the small room they were in were white except for a baby-girl-pink trim. There were only two pieces of furniture in the room: the small wooden chair that Gary had to carry in from the lobby and the small hospital bed that Staci now lay in. The floor was hard cement, sloping toward the drain in the middle of the room.

Gary sat with his face buried in his hands. It was the first time he had been this close to Staci since the ambulance left. His concentration had been on Sam. After the ambulance arrived, he called Marti and drove Sam over to his assistant's house to spend the night. Gary arrived at the hospital and watched a nurse insert a long tube down her throat. He saw the doctor begin to pump charcoal into her stomach, and he turned away to wait in the lobby.

The EMT had asked if he had wanted to go with Staci in the ambulance. The answer Gary gave was unusually cold. He could not help it. Being a father was all that mattered now. The role of husband was coming to a close.

Everything he had done in his life had led him to this moment. It depressed him beyond measure to know that despite all his planning in life he sat here next to the bed of a woman he no longer loved, who might have truly never loved, and dwelled on the horrifying moments of the night. The nightmare of the evening haunted him. He was disgusted by his thoughts. Having studied the law for years, having given an oath to follow the law, and having spent his whole career working within the law, he found himself contemplating, not taking a life per se but sitting idly by and watching life slip away without taking action. Was there a difference in actively killing someone with your actions and watching someone slip away into nothingness when you could prevent it?

Staci hadn't moved in the half hour that Gary sat next to her. He had left messages for her mother and father, not being able to get a hold of her family hours away. He stood up, no longer able to fake his concern. He knew where his relationship with Staci was headed, and it had come to a close. Whether she knew it or not at this point, for Gary it had ended.

As he walked out of the care facility, he signed out and asked the lady at the front desk to call him if her condition improved. As cold as he felt about her, he wasn't heartless. A large portion of his life had been wasted on her, and she had no one else around.

He got into the car and registered the time, 5:30 a.m. He texted Marti and asked her to bring Sam to the office with her in the morning. Marti's granddaughter and Sam had probably been up late into the night playing.

He hadn't slept all night but didn't think he could. As he came to a red light, he turned on his left blinker and then thought better of it. He had to do it and get it over with. It had to be now. Now was the time to strike, while the iron was hot as they say. And if he got lost in the scuttle of the day, he might not get to it right away.

He parked at his office, the sun beginning to show over the top of the hills. He went into the office, walking with a purpose. He turned on the computer, sat down abruptly, and opened the word processor with a pleading template and began to write.

In the Circuit Court of the State of Oregon
County of Klamath

Gary Alan Tornow,	PETITION FOR
	DISSOLUTION OF
Petitioner.	MARRIAGE
Staci Marie Tornow,	
Respondent.	

As he typed, his mind went numb. He went from typing the petition for himself to trying to do it for a client. He pretended that this was someone he didn't know personally. He began to think of what he would do and say. As stupid as it seemed, it made it easier on him. It made it easier to imagine this faceless person with these problems. These fucked-up problems.

He finished the petition in what seemed like minutes, but he looked up and it had been a half hour. He looked at it and then saw a picture of him and Sam in the corner of his eye. Normally, he would advise his client to get a restraining order or an immediate danger order. But he didn't know if he could go that far in his personal life. It scared him to get all this out there. This was going to get very public very fast. People he knew in the courthouse would know what he went daily. Would it change their opinion on him?

It didn't matter; he needed to do something. He thought about his prospects and decided that the restraining order would be best. In one swoop, she would be out of the house and away from Sam and him.

He sat in the chair and tried not to doze off. He thought about the prospects of going to the courthouse in the morning and filling out the restraining order paperwork. He thought about the court-house having to find a "conflict" judge, one he hadn't appeared in front of regularly. He thought of walking in and explaining his story and then having it spread like wildfire around the courthouse. He looked back at the nameless people in the crowd laughing at him. He saw Veronica Sanders almost choking on her ridicule. He saw Victoria Wampach pointing at him as she snorted with laughter. Then he saw Katelyn looking at him. Not laughing. Not pointing. Not joining the mocking in any way. She had a tear running down her face. Her dark eyes met his and she mouthed to him, "I'm here."

"Jesus, you look like shit!" Marti brought in his coffee, and Gary woke with a start. "Sam's in the play area with his cars. That kid has been through the ringer. What happened last night?"

"It's a long story. She's nuts, and I don't think I can do this anymore." He handed Marti the petition.

Marti sighed. "I'll get it filed. You okay?"

"I'm going down to get a restraining order. I gotta put a stop to this madness. I gotta move on. If not for me, for Sam." The night had brought him a long way. The thin thread that kept his marriage together had snapped. The fact that it was abundantly clear that Sam would no longer be safe in any way with Staci put everything into perspective. Gary had always believed that the two of them together, even if she was inadequate as a mother in almost every single way, was better for Sam somehow.

"Okay, um . . ." Marti had picked up his calendar and began to look through it. "It doesn't look like you have anything this morning. I'll watch Sam. Do you mind if I keep the doors closed until you get back?"

"Please do." Gary didn't like some of his clientele being around the office when Sam was there and especially when he wasn't.

Gary resigned himself to what he must do. He grabbed his spare suit out of the closet in the office hallway and changed in the bathroom before heading to his car.

As he drove to the courthouse, he looked at all the people on the sidewalk not going through a divorce. He envied them. He envied them not because he was sad about his relationship with Staci coming to an end but because the amount of chaos that was in his life was consuming. It was exhausting beyond measure.

Gary's mind began to dig deeper though. He thought about the people on the sidewalk and then thought about the persona he put on every day. He thought about the way he had told people how happy he was. He thought about how shocked everybody he knew would be about the things that had happened in his house.

Realization hit him that most of them, or most likely all of them, were miserable in some fashion. That woman over on the corner? Her husband was probably out fucking a hooker. The old man waiting in line for coffee? His children probably hadn't called him in months. The man driving that bus? He probably can't get an erection. The children playing on the playground during recess? Half of them probably had parents who barely paid attention to them. Some of them had parents who were drunks, some of them struggled to make friends, some were beaten every night, and some faced something much worse when they went home.

He parked his car and made his way to the courthouse. He walked through security without checking in, as he always had, even though he wasn't here for business. He walked toward the clerk's office.

The paperwork he had grabbed was the same he had filled out on other people's behalf dozens of times. He turned it into the clerk and went to wait in the lobby area.

"Mr. Tornow?" The clerk walked out to speak to him. "I spoke to Judge Oswald, who is the duty judge this week. She told me we need a conflict judge. We have arranged for a video hearing with a judge in Lake County. Go ahead and come with me."

"Okay" was the only word that Gary managed to get out. He walked behind her and into one of the courtrooms.

"Hi, Gary," Danielle, Judge Abraham's clerk, greeted him. "You doing okay?" She said the last words with the delicacy that one would normally reserve for speaking to a loved one on their deathbed.

It was worse than Gary had thought. He had not been met with shock but with sadness. Danielle, and likely the rest of the legal community now that Gary thought about it, had either seen through the issues he was having, had seen through the persona he put on, or they had come to the realization long ago that he had reached in the car. The realization that not only is the world not perfect, but the lines of earth and hell blurred more than the lines of heaven and earth.

That evil, hurt, and despair plagued the hearts of all men. That his suffering was not unique to him.

"I don't know, to be honest," he told Danielle.

She put her hand on his shoulder in a reassuring manner. Danielle was likely in her early sixties. Gary was astonished at the comfort it gave him. Like the hug of a grandmother. It gave him strength.

"I didn't think it would ever come to this," Gary said, looking everywhere but at her.

Danielle was looking at him, trying to catch his eye. Gary looked up at her. Danielle sighed. "No one ever does. But that's the reason we exist. If everyone always knew how things were going to go, then you would be out of a job." She smiled warmly at him. Danielle walked back to her computer and sat down. Gary took her lead, realizing the hearing was about to begin.

Gary took a seat at one of the courtroom tables. Danielle had turned the television on from her seat and the connection began to upload.

"Can everyone hear me?" the judge said over the video.

"Yes," Gary responded.

"Okay, this is Judge Jacob Bushong in Klamath County case number 15CV34867, a Family Abuse Prevention Act petition. Petitioner Gary Tornow is present in the courtroom. Mr. Tornow, please raise your right hand, and I'll swear you in." Gary raised his hand. "Under the penalty of perjury, do you swear to tell the truth, the whole truth, and nothing but the truth?" The judge read the oath, still having not looked up at Gary since he showed up on the screen.

"Yes," Gary recited.

"Mr. Tornow, the clerk sent me a copy of the petition via fax. Do you swear that the contents of the petition are accurate?"

"Yes," Gary recited again. The usual course of a restraining order hearing would have had the petitioner talking about the issues within the petition. However, as Gary had seen before with other lawyers that had struggles in their lives, his word went without question.

"Okay, well, I've reviewed the order. The facts are sufficient to grant the order for your protection. But the problem is parenting time. I understand that this happened in front of your son and that your wife is currently in a mental health facility, but upon her release, I think it is important that we accommodate some parenting time. Does she have anyone that can supervise her parenting time?"

Gary thought. "She doesn't have any family in the area. I know her mother would be willing to, but she lives five hours away."

"Okay, well, here is what I'm going to do," the judge began, "I'm going to grant her eight hours of supervised time per week to be completed with a supervisor of your choice. I would like the visits to be somewhat frequent, every couple of days or so. But if you can't find a supervisor on a regular basis, then larger chunks will have to work. Good luck, Mr. Tornow." And with that, the hearing ended abruptly.

The television shut off. Danielle smiled at him as she left the room. Alone in the courtroom, the shock of the events finally got to. Gary lowered his head into his hands and began to sob loudly.

CHAPTER 11

● ● ● ● ● ●

A Liberating Shower, a Wedgie, and Public Castration

The cool breeze through his hair put him in a state of relaxation that he rarely was able to feel. The sound of the ocean waves indulged his senses. "Daddy, don't put that there!" Gary had fumbled the sandcastle bucket and poured some of it in his moat. The mighty castle looked more like the ruins of a pitiful civilization than the foundation of a great kingdom. But a sandcastle built by a three-year-old and a lawyer who could barely hit a nail with a hammer was never going in the Smithsonian.

When he had arrived back at his office, Gary checked his calendar. He didn't have court for the rest of the week. Katelyn's trial on the following Tuesday was his next in court appearance. The only appointment he had to keep in the next coming days was a preparation appointment with Katelyn that wasn't scheduled for a couple of days. Gary had instructed Marti to clear his calendar of the other appointments and to close the office for a couple of days. The marginal amount of business he might lose was nothing to the mind he had lost. He needed time to compute everything that had happened.

He went immediately from his office parking lot home to pack and straight off to seaside. The sand, the smell of the saltwater, and the company of the only person in the world he truly loved gave him the environment he needed to reboot. The devastation of the last few days had left Gary in a place mentally where he could never successfully try a case. His strength? Waning. His confidence? Gone. His self-esteem? Well . . . he wasn't sure if he had that to begin with.

"Sam, grab some of the sand we dug up. Let's get these walls higher." They piled the sand higher and higher between the turrets. The moat that they had dug was without water. Sam had continued to try to fill it with some standing water near the area they were building the fortress. The water kept soaking back into the sand. The broken sand dollars and shells they had gathered in the morning were left forgotten in the excitement of the castle. "Let's use these in the castle," he told Sam, and they began to stick them into the walls.

They grabbed some driftwood on the shoreline and began to stack it near the castle, about five feet away. The sun was slowly setting on the horizon. Although the wind chill made it much colder than the August evening should be. Most of the people they saw along the shore were still wearing shorts.

Gary took a towel and wiped off Sam's hands and feet. He took the blanket he had brought down from the hotel and placed part of it on the ground for Sam to sit on. "Can you waffle me in it, Daddy?" Sam asked him. It was their word for wrapping it around him. Gary smiled and wrapped it around him.

Gary had grabbed two lighters from the mini mart down the road earlier. He took one out of his pocket and ripped off the top. He poured the fluid onto the small pile of driftwood they had assembled. He then took the other lighter and lit a napkin. He threw the napkin on to the now highly flammable wood, and the fire erupted.

He took a seat next to Sam and placed his arm around him. He squeezed Sam's shoulder, and they sat in near silence for some time. As the sun began to dim, Sam began to ask about the various lights in the distance. "Well, that is probably a little kid building a fire in Japan," was one of the go-to comments Gary would make. Sam chuckled each time he made the joke.

The effects of the past days had not yet seemed to weigh on Sam. He had not yet asked about his mother. Then again, Gary taking Sam away for a couple of days was not unheard of. He had from time to time taken Sam to see his parents in Portland without Staci's company.

Then as Gary's thoughts dug deeper, he began to realize that this wasn't necessarily a good thing. Most children would be affected in some way by the brutal events. But not Sam. And why? Because of the shit he had already gone through at three. His mother not being there was nothing new. The yelling was nothing new. The suicidal, homicidal, psychopathic behavior displayed by Staci certainly wasn't unique to the night.

Gary continued to gaze into the fire, and Sam began to lean closer to him. He had always heard the phrase "You will never know love until you have children." Truer words had never been spoken. True love didn't seem to exist between a man and a woman. That was reserved for parent and child. A bond that could both be so loose that it could destroy life or so tight that it could be the resolve that kept one alive.

Gary had realized at that point that Sam had drifted off. Gary's only true feelings of happiness, of joy, of laughter came from Sam. Not clients. Not other attorneys. Certainly not Staci. In his mind, Gary's mind replayed watching his son playing with action figures when he was just two. Sam had one of the ninjas kick the other, only to need to go to the bathroom and get a Band-Aid for the injured action figure afterward.

He recalled a time when Sam had just begun potty training. Gary had been cleaning dishes in the kitchen, Staci was of course in the basement, and Gary heard Sam begin to scream. Sam wasn't a very good talker yet, and he just kept pointing behind himself. It took well over two minutes for Gary to realize that, Sam being a novice at big boy underwear, had been highly alarmed by his first wedgie.

Gary remembered a trial he had when Sam was about four months old. He remembered the night before, being exhausted, but waking up with Sam and rocking him back to sleep with a bottle. Gary had drifted in and out of sleep, and although he had never slept worse, the refreshment of having him in his arms all night made him more ready than he had ever been.

The remembered day Sam was born and the promise he made in his heart then and there. He promised Sam that he would always do what was best for him. It hardened his resolve. Gary knew that he was right to take Sam. He was right to move on in life.

Slowly, the fire began to burn to the ground. Gary put Sam in his arms and began to walk back to the hotel. They were on the first floor. Gary slid open the sliding glass door and walked Sam straight to the bed and tucked him in. Already asleep or not, it didn't matter, as Gary began to sing his nighttime song. "Hey, okay, we had another fantastic day, and now it's time to say . . . goodnight . . ." A small tear began to form in the corner of Gary's right eye. "'Cause we got places to go, bubbles to blow, stories to share, and dreams to grow, so goodnight . . ." He kissed Sam on the forehead.

Gary walked into the bathroom to take a shower. He smiled at himself in the bathroom. Relief and happiness overwhelmed him. Feelings that he hadn't had for so long that hadn't been sure he was still capable of them. He turned on the shower and stepped in and immediately sat down, allowing the hot water to flood onto his chest. He closed his eyes, smiling and trying not to drift off. Staci had always said it was stupid. But this place, this exact hotel, was where his odd habit had begun.

As a child, Gary didn't grow up with middle-class parents. His parents struggled most of his life. Both were well educated and doing well, but his mother was young and hadn't completed her psychology degree until he was twelve years old. Their family trips had always been to the beach. They never had money to eat out with, so they always brought a cooler full of sandwich stuff.

Until he was twelve and his parents could finally afford to move into a newer house, he had been without a shower. He took baths every day as a child until that point, except at the beach. It seemed foolish now, but he had thought that showers were for rich people. He would sit in the shower for hours, with the luxury of the never-ending hot water supply. Later on in life, he did so at home occasionally, but of course, only until the hot water ran out. Staci always hated the habit, and by the time they were married, Gary had stopped the ritual for good.

Now, he was free to do his nostalgic act. It was silly. It was childish. But it was liberating. It was a simple act of defiance that empowered Gary. Gary felt like maybe him doing this was evidence that the good person he felt he left behind before Staci, before law school, before all the justifications for the things he had to do for work in defending the rights of people who deserved to be publicly castrated and allowed to bleed to death . . . well, maybe that person was still there. Maybe that person, who was capable of emotional growth, could be nurtured again. This small act of rebellion against the shackles of Staci made him feel like he could look for love and that maybe, just maybe, he might actually be worthy of it.

It simultaneously made Gary happier in some ways than he ever had been and sadder. He could make his life outside of his office once again worthwhile. But the realization that Staci's treatment of him made him feel worthless, unworthy of love, unworthy of happiness, unworthy of affection . . . he just couldn't form the words in his mind. It was too much.

It was never that he needed love from someone else. He needed to love himself, and the worst things that Staci had done to him didn't make him hate her but hate himself.

CHAPTER 12

● ● ● ● ● ● ●

Collision

"He really hasn't said that much to him. He's been seeing Steve since just a couple days after we first met. I'm not sure exactly why, but he won't open up." Katelyn was looking down, not making eye contact with Gary. It was as if she was terrified to hear what he had to say about it.

"It doesn't matter. He'll get fifty-fifty over my dead body. He hasn't been nearly the father Brandon deserves." Katelyn's mother, Jerry, had been upset the moment that Gary had said he really didn't like the odds of winning the trial without more evidence.

"If we go to fifty-fifty, it isn't the end. It doesn't mean that Brandon can't keep seeing Steve. It doesn't mean that you have to lie down and not fight anymore. But I don't see this going our way. You guys testifying about what you have heard isn't going to be enough, at least I don't think it is going to be," Gary said with a heavy heart and shaky voice. It was hard to tell Katelyn the truth about her case, but the evidence simply hadn't developed favorably.

"I still think that"—Katelyn paused—"well, I need to try to fight for Brandon. I'm his mother, and I can't let this happen to him. He needs me, and I just hope the judge sees it."

Jerry had looked at her phone for long periods periodically throughout the meeting. She appeared to be reading a text, "Sweetie, your sister needs to be picked up from school. I'm going to have to leave. Just let me know what you want to do." Jerry left the room, and Katelyn and Gary found themselves alone.

"Honestly, is this about Brandon or your mom?" Gary raised his right eyebrow and stared at Katelyn.

"You've met her, what do you think? Look, I want Brandon full-time. But I'm not an idiot. I know what is going to happen if we fight this. I just . . . I guess I didn't think he would ever want him full-time. It's weird. I never thought he'd want to be a dad. It's like he is doing it because of the way we ended." Katelyn shrugged.

"I just can't tell you how bad of an idea I think that this is. We have to think about future litigation here, as well. You're going to look petty. We already know that it is going to come out bad, so why do it? The other issue is that the law for custody contains an attorney fees provision. I don't think that the judge would do it, but it is possible that you could have to pay a portion of his attorney fees. It doesn't happen that often, but if the judge thinks you are being unreasonable, it is possible."

Gary looked at Katelyn with piercing analysis. Her eyes were the same as the first time he met her, not as he had come to know her. There was defeat in her eyes. Her brown hair flowed down past her shoulders. The shirt she was wearing showed more of her prodigious breast than any shirt she had ever worn in front of him. It was a green low-cut tank top. It was the kind of shirt that women wore so men would look at them even though men were never supposed to look, but of course, men were to pretend not to know that. Was it for his benefit? He shook his head.

"Anyways, what do you want to do? Adam Rose has proposed some judgment terms, and they are reasonable if we are going to a fifty-fifty plan. He makes more money so that you will still get a chunk of child support. The first right of refusal is in play, which means that if he needs child care for any reason, you get first dibs, and . . . are you okay?"

The look on Katelyn's face was chalk white. A tear began to slowly form on the outside of her left eye. Then all of a sudden, her tears broke free. She sat there with her eyes locked on Gary and sobbed.

"It's not fair. I don't get it. I get crap from all my family for leaving Paul when we had a child, but I didn't have an ounce of love for him. I don't understand love. It's like . . . it's like I'm not supposed to love anyone except Brandon. Paul sat around and watched videos of tractors on the internet all night. Joey gets so drunk at night that the only thing he ever wants to do is have sex, but then he can't even get up for it with only whiskey in his veins. It's not fair that I have to fight over Brandon, the only person in this world who loves me. Even my mother doesn't give a flying fuck."

"She was here for you," Gary jumped in and immediately regretted it.

"You are mistaking blind spite for care. She doesn't care about whether I come out of this feeling right or not. She cares about winning. She cares about never being wrong. She always hated Paul. Even when I did care about him, she never gave him the time of day. Actually, it was really stupid why. She overheard us on the phone. Paul said someone was a bitch, I don't even remember who. Might have been a teacher. Anyways, my mom heard it and thought that he was calling her a bitch. Ever since then, she has been a bitter cunt to him. We even dated for two years after that." Katelyn had one from sad to furious in seconds.

"Someone is out there for you. I mean, look, I get it. Sam to me is everything, and I can't imagine love outside of him because no one has really ever shown me love outside of him. I mean"—he paused and pondered his words—"my parents are great and have been great. But it is different. I understand how you feel about your mom, but even if she was perfect, it wouldn't fill that void," Gary hesitated, choosing his next words carefully. "You and Joey are . . ."

"Complicated," Katelyn finished the sentence. "I don't love him, but he is good to Brandon. I thought that was enough. For a while it was. Then he started drinking more and more. Now, well, it's just different. It was never great. It was just good enough to hold on. Kind of like when someone doesn't really like a job, but they need their job and they put in just enough effort not to fuck it up and get fired, ya know? That is what it feels like from him. Just enough effort and attention to me for me not to throw him on his sorry ass."

"How is it that two people living two very different lives can have so much in common?" Gary smiled at Katelyn for the first time during this exchange. "We both have sons, the same age practically. We have failed love lives. Feel rejection around us. It is bizarre."

Gary hesitated and got up from his desk chair and moved around the desk. He pulled the chair next to Katelyn around and turned it toward her. He sat down and looked at her.

"It's going to happen for you," Gary started, and Katelyn laughed cynically.

"Why? How can you possibly know that?" she said with exasperation and a smile at the same time. "How in the fucking world can you of all people be such a positive Polly? You deal with child rapists, a crazy wife, and then bullshit like mine all day. How the fucking hell can you sit here and tell me that it is going to happen?" She stared at him, half grinning. Something about the dark view they both had of life made both of them glow; Gary knew it. He drew such comfort by the truth in her words but also knew what he hoped for.

"It's supposed to happen for everyone. And most of those child rapists go to prison despite my efforts. As long as their checks clear, them going to prison makes the streets safer for my kid. My crazy 'wife' and I have a pending divorce. And bullshit like yours, while it sucks, it creates a brighter future for your kid. And quite frankly, your particular bullshit is the most fun I have outside of time with my son. So yes, I am a positive fucking Polly."

"Good Lord. God must have shoved a buttload of rainbows in you after putting in the drops of evil to make you a lawyer." Katelyn paused. "Wait, pending divorce? When did that happen?" Katelyn's look turned to one of concern.

Gary took a deep breath. "Okay, do you remember the other night when we ran into each other?" Katelyn nodded.

"Of course. Brandon won't stop talking about it."

"Well, before we ran into each other, I had gotten home, and Sam was alone."

"Like alone alone?" Katelyn asked.

"Alone alone. I couldn't find Staci anywhere. Sam was sitting alone in front of the TV when I walked in. He was starving. And he acted like it wasn't something that was out of the ordinary. So anyways, he asked for spaghetti. So we went out to get it and ran into you."

"Shit, what the hell happened when you got home?" Katelyn questioned.

"Hell. I'm not sure how to even explain it. It happened so damn fast. She came at me, hitting me. I put Sam down, and I don't know what he saw. But she thought I was cheating on her with someone, and she grabbed my phone. She tried to flush it down the toilet, and god, it happened so quickly . . ." Gary hesitated again and looked at the ceiling.

"Jeez, then what?" Katelyn was captivated by the drama.

"It is all such a blur now. She hit me in the head, and quite frankly, I don't remember. I remember feeling the blood, and god, it hurt. Then I saw Sam. And I don't know what he saw." Gary stopped, but this time Katelyn didn't say anything. Gary had slumped down and placed his elbows on his thighs and his hands in his lap. Katelyn reached her right hand over and touched his shoulder. Gary caught her perfume in the air and felt drunk off it instantly.

He carried on. "Apparently, during it all, she grabbed some pills and ran down to the basement. I, well, I didn't follow her right away. I made sure Sam was okay. I thought about not following her and helping her at all. But I did. Then I found her. She had taken a bunch of the pills. I just followed the 911 operator's instructions from there."

"Where is she now?" Katelyn inquired.

"Phoenix House. They still haven't released her. It was a close call. Her mother is supposed to pick her up tomorrow actually. She is supposed to see Sam at some point in the next few days. Her parenting time is supervised through a restraining order for now."

"How did her mom react?"

"Like any parent would. Concerned for her daughter, taking her side, whatever crazy-ass side that might be. I haven't talked to Staci since that night though, at least with her conscious." Gary looked at Katelyn. She had tears in her eyes again. "You've shed enough tears already, don't use what you have left on me."

Katelyn wiped her eyes with a tissue from Gary's desk. "I don't know how you are so strong. I feel like I'm falling apart over the bullshit. And you are doing this kind of job with this sort of stress, and it doesn't show. I don't get it. It's amazing how you can deal with all this."

Without thinking, he put his right hand on her knee. "Somehow I've always managed to pull through." Now, tears began to fill Gary's eyes.

"You too, huh?" Katelyn sniffled tears back. She stood up and got next to Gary's chair on the left hand side and hugged him. With one arm. Gary got up and hugged her back, with one arm as well. Katelyn's second arm wrapped around him then, and Gary followed suit. Her head was against his chest. He could feel the tears going through his shirt to his chest. Katelyn could no doubt hear his heart's thunderous beats due to her being in his arms. He looked down at her brown hair and realized how much he had wanted this and yet how wrong it felt at the same time. He knew he couldn't. He wanted her more than anything but couldn't jeopardize Sam's future.

Katelyn looked up at him. Tears in her eyes but a smile on her lips. His resolve to do the right thing melted instantly. He bent down and put his lips to hers. He sensed surprise at first, and then her head tilted slightly to the left, and her lips began to move with fiery passion. Her hands grasped the back of his shirt and pushed him in closer to her. Gary's left hand was in the lower part of her back, and he moved his right hand up to her cheek and held her face as they embraced.

Then all of a sudden, she said, "I know we can't. We just can't. I know you're my lawyer, and I know we can't do this. Look, I'm sorry. I shouldn't . . . I don't . . . I . . ." Gary just looked at her and nodded.

"I know. Look. This is almost over. Maybe sometime down the road, when life isn't so complicated and I'm not your lawyer anymore. I just. I know that we have a connection. I don't know what it is. Maybe it is because of all of this time for your case, maybe it is our kids in common, but I don't know."

"I didn't think you felt it. It's weird. I barely know you, and you are constantly on my mind. You have no idea how good it felt to go to the bar with someone and just have fun." She sniffled. "I almost kissed you that night. We didn't even know each other except for the shitty set of circumstances we were in. And it was like a magnet." Katelyn ended and smiled at him.

"I never thought . . ." Gary paused. "I'm not good-looking, and you are beautiful. I just never thought . . ."

"Oh stop with that crap," She actually laughed. "First off, you are good-looking, don't say that again. But it goes beyond that. And I know I have to walk away from it . . ." she hesitated. "But I don't think I can. I don't want to walk out that door and this just go away."

"It won't, I promise." Gary grabbed her hand and kissed it.

"How are you so perfect? It's like you understand exactly what I need." She smiled at him and embraced him again. He felt her tears on his chest again.

"I know we barely know each other," Gary said. "And maybe that is why something this risky needs to wait. To give it time to see how life unravels."

"Ya," Katelyn started, sniffling again. "You are right." She kept his hand in hers, and they made for the office door. "I guess this is it then?" She hugged him and opened the door, dropping his hand as the door opened. Marti wasn't at her desk. Something Gary had tried to arrange for this day. They walked to the door.

"I'll let his attorney know we have a settlement, and I'll have you come by in a few days to sign a judgment, okay?" Katelyn nodded.

Katelyn stopped at the door. She turned toward Gary. She looked at him with intense passion, and he felt a monster in his chest awaken. His heart pounded furiously. She took his hand again in hers and kissed him on the cheek. Katelyn made to go for the door, but he held onto her hand. He slowly pulled her back and moved in to her, kissing her plump lips again.

"I'll see you in a couple of days." Gary let her hand go.

"Fuck it," Katelyn stated, shrugging her shoulders. She put her hands on his waist and reached her head up and kissed him. She pushed him back into a chair in the waiting area. She startled herself on him and continued to kiss him.

Neither of them spoke. Gary moved his hands from the back of her head down her back and slowly inch by inch down to her buttocks, where her hair ended. She moved her lips from his mouth to his neck. Gary ran his hands through her hair and began to neck her as well. He then moved his hands from her hair to her back where her tank top was slowly moving upward. He grabbed the bottom and slowly pulled it up. She sat up and allowed him to move the shirt over her head and once again locked her lips on his. He moved his hands to her bra strap and unhooked it in one swift motion. Her breasts fell free, and Katelyn began to kiss his neck again. She pulled on his shirt and began to lift it over Gary's head.

She pulled away and ran her hands up and down his chest. Gary grabbed her back and pushed her while sitting up toward him. He took her right nipple in his mouth, and she arched herself backward in passion. He felt her right hand move toward his waistline and slowly move over his manhood. He felt her undo his belt and button.

Katelyn began kissing him again. She then moved to his neck, his chest, his stomach, and slowly toward his waist. He ran his hands through her hair as her head moved toward his lap. He closed his eyes, not believing any of this happened. He felt, rather than saw, her take his engorged manhood into her mouth. It was pure ecstasy. He looked down at her. And she fixed her eyes on him as she worked.

He pulled up on her, and she moved up toward him again. He shook free the legs that still had part of his pants on them. He grabbed her hips and moved his hands slowly to undo her pants as she kissed him. He pulled them down slowly, along with her thong, and moved them to her knees. She had grabbed his manhood and began moving her hand.

He picked her up in one swoop and moved her to the carpet floor. He continued kissing her passionately, and he lay idle on top of her. She moved her hands to his face, framing his head as she kissed him. He slowly entered her, and she moaned with pleasure.

CHAPTER 13

● ● ● ● ● ● ●

Aftershock

The emotions going through Gary were hard to process. He thought about how rare it must be for a person to experience the entire spectrum of human emotions within minutes. The prevailing emotion was joy beyond any conceivable measurement. But there was regret for his failed attempt at marriage with Staci, no matter the shattered state it had been in for years. Sadness for the position it put his son in as a broken home was what he had been working so hard to avoid despite the misery it caused him. Overwhelming lust that consumed as nothing had consumed him before. Love, at least he thought, or perhaps hoped as he wasn't quite sure what to think of love.

They had sat in his office after they climaxed simultaneously for about a half hour, holding each other. For the majority of the time, they didn't say anything, both of them trying to figure out what they had done. When they both had finally realized that they needed to relieve their babysitters, they dressed slowly, and Katelyn made her way for the door. The goodnight kiss was full of more passion than any kiss Gary had ever experienced. They had agreed that seeing each other regularly couldn't happen until things in life settled down, but Katelyn told Gary to call her in a few days, and they could figure out somewhere safe to meet.

Which brought Gary to the emotion of hate. There was self-disgust pumping through his veins at a rapid pace. In law school, Gary's ethics teacher had used a slideshow on the first day and lectured, not on the finer points of the ethical practice of law but on those violations that reached above others. The violations that could cause one to lose the right to practice law. He summed it up on the first slideshow with three rules: (1) don't screw your clients, (2) don't screw your clients, and (3) don't screw your clients. The first point was don't screw your clients by stealing from them; always be cautious with their money. The second one was do not screw them by being neglectful. Even if you didn't know exactly how to solve a problem, giving the problem attention was important. The last one was literal and the class had howled with laughter as the slideshow ran through: "Engage in coitus, intercourse, fornication, fuck, nail, screw, nookie, or make whoopee with a client." Apparently, this ethics class hadn't stuck with Gary as well as he thought it had.

He despised himself over his moment of lust that could cost him everything. His livelihood. Sam's future. Everything he had worked for could be flushed down the shitter if anyone found out. He realized that doing this meant a high level of commitment to Katelyn without really knowing her. Admittedly, he never knew that the feeling he had for her existed. But if it ever went south, he knew that his license to practice law could be in jeopardy. It didn't worry him though. Something about Katelyn made him feel comfort, and his usual doomsday scenario analyzing of a situation didn't faze him for once.

He had picked Sam up from the daycare that he had made arrangements with earlier in the week. It was Sam's first time in daycare. Now he had to explain what was going on with his mother. Now he had to explain why Staci wasn't living with them anymore. Why his grandmother had to come to town for his mother to get time with him. He pulled into a restaurant parking lot and stopped and turned off the engine. His favorite burger joint. Not fast food. It was greasy, 'merican killin', calorie-stacking, melting-cheese goodness.

"Dad, I want a milkshake! Butterscotch!" He always got excite to get his milkshake.

"Sure, buddy."

Gary ordered their usual meal. One large bacon burger with extra cheese and ketchup, one kid's burger with everything, family-sized French fry basket, butterscotch milkshake, and cola. He hadn't even had to order before the lady taking the order smiled and began to write down the order.

They ate in silence for a while. Gary was trying to figure out what exactly to say when Sam said, "Daddy, is Mommy in the big kid corner?"

"What do you mean, little buddy?" Gary was puzzled.

"I asked Mommy one day what happens when adults are bad. Mommy told me they go to a corner like little kids, but it's like a big building."

"No, buddy. Mommy is . . ." Gary fished for the word. "Mommy is sick. She isn't feeling well. And so she isn't going to be at home anymore."

"But she was bad." Sam looked at him in a matter-of-fact manner.

"Yes, son, she was bad." Gary sighed. "What did you see?"

"She hit you. She hurt your head." Sam took a bite of his burger.

"Well, Sam, Daddy decided to not put Mommy in the corner," he continued with the analogy. "But Daddy knew she needed help, so he took Mommy to the doctor."

"Oh." Sam seemed to be thinking. "What kind of doctor, Daddy?"

"One that helps someone with the way they think," Gary answered.

"Like a teacher?"

"No, not like a teacher," Gary began. Sam was trying to ratio-nalize this in a way that made sense in his world. "Well, ya, buddy, like a teacher. Not a teacher, but a doctor that teaches things."

Sam sat in silence for a few moments. "Where is Mommy going to sleep?"

"Daddy is going to pay for Mommy to have an apartment. It's like a small house. She will sleep there. You'll get to see it soon. You'll see your Mommy tomorrow."

"Will I see her small house tomorrow?" Sam asked.

"No, little buddy. Your Grandma Hibbard is going to come down for a while tomorrow. Isn't that cool?"

"Grammy is coming! Daddy, can we go to pizza like last time? I want to play that car game?"

"Buddy, Daddy isn't going to be there. You just get time with Grammy and Mommy, but Daddy will give Grammy some money so that she can take you guys, okay?"

"But you play the car game with me," Sam added with a look of disappointment.

"I bet Mommy will this time, okay?" Gary ended.

Sam nodded.

Later that evening, after Gary put Sam to bed, Gary sat down and put on a recorded episode of *Star Trek: The Next Generation*. Having arrived from the beach earlier that morning, this was the first night he had spent in the home without Staci. The events of the last week hung heavy with him, but there was an astronomical relief as well. He could watch *Star Trek* without the fear of being ridiculed, yelled at, threatened, struck, stabbed, shot . . . Jesus, was this how normal people lived? He could enjoy the things that made him who he was.

It was a combination of not being under Staci's mercy and the emotion from his connection with Katelyn going through him that liberated his mood. It wasn't pitiful to fall asleep to *Star Trek* every night; it was quirky. It wasn't stupid to love books about teenage wizards and an awesome school they go to. It wasn't stupid to be him. That was different. He had spent so much time at home hating himself. Now, he really had a chance to appreciate home. Now, he could share these things with Sam, maybe with Katelyn . . . although Star Trek might be a stretch.

He dozed off, smiling in his sleep.

When Gary awoke the next morning, Sam was sitting on the floor in front of the TV with it already on. Gary picked up his phone; it was only six thirty.

"Hi, buddy, why are you up so early?" Gary asked Sam.

"I get to see Mommy today!" Sam grinned.

Through this, Gary had to remember that as terrible of a person as she might be, it was Sam who needed to make his own conclusions about Staci. Sam needed his mother, as any little boy did. Inadequate or not, Gary had to encourage the relationship.

"Yes, you do, buddy! Let's jump in the bath. Your Grandma Hibbard is going to be over at about nine. We have time for breakfast and some games first, okay?" Gary said with excitement. Sam nodded vigorously and made his way to the bathroom.

Gary bathed Sam in a raging frenzy of bubbles and pirates. Well, plastic toy pirates. And Mr. Bubbles to be exact. After he dried Sam, Gary made them omelets, and they watched cartoons as they ate.

Gary dressed Sam, and Gary's heart began to sink. He would have to face his mother-in-law for the first time since this all happened. Gary wasn't sure what she did and didn't know. Amy had always been kind to Gary. But Gary knew that this was the kind of situation that no matter how much she liked him, Amy would choose Staci's side. It was natural. He had seen Amy at her worst too. Not against him. But when he was younger, against Staci. She was just as cold-hearted in the end as Staci, but she was practical. She knew who Gary was, and she knew how well he took care of Staci.

Gary heard the doorbell ring. "Okay, that's your grandma. Let's go say hi!" Gary put on the show.

"Okay!" Sam exclaimed and ran to the door.

Sam was about ten feet in front of Gary and turned around and smiled at him. Gary opened the door, and his mother-in-law was on the porch.

"Hi, Gary, can we talk for a few moments?"

"Sure, come in." Gary had made a gesture with his left hand for her to come and take a seat on the couch.

"Grammy, are you going to take me to Mommy?" Sam asked her.

"Yes, Sammy, but I need to have grown-up talk with your dad first. Will you go play in your room for a while?" Amy asked him.

Sam looked at Gary. "Go ahead, buddy. We will only be a few minutes." Sam ran off to his room.

"How is she?" Gary asked, thinking it would be cold-hearted not to ask.

"She is," Amy hesitated. "She is having a hard time understanding that you aren't going to let her come home. She's hurt, Gary. She wants to come back home." She spoke very frankly and harshly.

"I can't do that. I can't do that to me. I can't do that to Sam," Gary started, but Amy pushed in.

"To Sam?" she interrupted. "What is it doing to Sam?"

"Sam has seen more of us fighting at the age of three than I saw my parents do in eighteen years of growing up. It isn't healthy for him," Gary spoke with authority.

"He needs her, and she needs him," Amy spoke softly. She lost the edge to her voice. This was a plea, not a demand or even a request. This came straight down to begging.

"Yes, he does. What she needs isn't important. She's a grown woman. And it isn't about her, it is about him. I'm not taking him away, but she needs help. And . . ." Gary paused a moment. "It doesn't matter what she does to help herself, we are done."

"So someone else then?" Amy's sharp voice had returned.

"No, no one else," only half a lie. The decision to go through the divorce had been made well before Gary and Katelyn had made love.

"Look." Amy returned to her pleading voice, apparently satisfied that he wasn't fucking anyone. "I got her an apartment, like you asked. I'll leave the stuff here for you to pay for like you said you would. But well, I'll be in town again over next weekend. I have a three-day weekend, Friday through Sunday. I was wondering . . ."

"You want Sam?" Gary finished. "The order doesn't allow overnights, but . . ." Gary thought. "Okay, okay, look, if she agrees not to challenge the restraining order, she can have overnights with you in town. That's fine. She isn't going to get much time when you aren't around. But Sam has to be in whatever room you are in overnight, and you have to have full supervision all day, deal?"

Amy nodded. A tear ran down Amy's left check. Gary stood up, moving toward Sam's room to get him. He was abruptly stopped, and Amy embraced him.

CHAPTER 14

Filet Mignon

"I'm just saying that all men are pigs when it comes down to it. That's all I'm saying. No, I'm not surprised that it wasn't a one-time thing because of the connection I felt. But yes, the thought passed through me, I can't lie about it," Katelyn said emphatically.

"I get it, I had the same insecurities," Gary started. "But I'm not like that."

"Oh please, all men are *like* that. You really didn't think about fucking a bunch of different women after you knew you were leaving Staci? I mean, you had been married for all those years and were always faithful. So I'm just surprised that you wanted to jump into another relationship."

"I didn't think about it like that. I had been lonely for a long time. And quite frankly, 'fucking' a bunch of different women may be most men's dream, but not mine. I want to be happy. And I don't think that is how it is done."

"Every man wants to be a player. Every man wants a bunch of different women. You are weird, that is all I have to say." She giggled. "Every man wants to be Gene Simmons or Derek Jeter or Mick Jagger or Justin Bieber . . ."

"Justin Bieber?" Gary rolled his eyes.

"Don't be a jealous, Bieber hater. He is rich, good-looking, and fucks Selena Gomez on a regular basis," Katelyn argued.

Gary chuckled. "Okay, maybe, but still. Gene Simmons though? Really? He has slept with 5 million women. You make three women for me. That is over-fucking-whelming."

"Are you saying that if given the opportunity, you wouldn't want to?" Katelyn raised her eyebrows, daring him to say no.

"I'd prefer it if my genitals don't just fall off some day. Let me tell you a little story about Gene Simmons. About ten years ago, and mind you he was old ten years ago, he was on tour. He slept with Miss America. Not a washed-up Miss America, not a Miss America who just turned thirty, but the reigning Miss America. A glorious feat if using your pig standards." Gary smiled at Katelyn. "But the next night, a member of the road crew saw Gene Simmons go into a restroom with a woman who was a hot mess, so gross the road crew wouldn't touch her. *Then* the next night, the road crew member is sitting in the bar in a hotel. He sees Gene Simmons practically dragging a large woman across the lobby toward the elevator. The road crew member walked out of the bar and looked toward the elevator. He saw the large woman leaning on the wall of the elevator, and Gene Simmons fold his arms standing tall and mouths 'Oh yeah' to the road crew member."

"So he went hog hunting? Are you saying you wouldn't sleep with a woman who was overweight?" Katelyn raised her eyebrows.

"Who is the pig now?" Gary smiled at her. "You want me to continue, or are you going to make fun of my story some more?"

"Continue. But would you?"

"Generally speaking, I don't operate heavy machinery. But if I loved her, it wouldn't matter," Gary added.

"So you'd operate a backhoe as long as you loved her, I get it." She grinned at him.

Gary rolled his eyes again. "Anyways, the road crew member asked Gene Simmons the next morning if he slept with the woman. Gene said, 'Of course.' The road crew guy said, 'You slept with Miss America two nights ago. Then you drag a street walker into a toilet and big bad woman into an elevator the next couple of nights. What gives?' Gene looked at him and said, 'Son, you can't eat filet mignon every night. Sometimes, you gotta eat off the dollar menu."

Katelyn had just taken a drink of soda and squirted most it out of her nose. "Um, okay, so what exactly is the moral of your story of promiscuity?"

"The moral? I feel like I had to eat off the dollar menu enough for a lifetime. I'm only up for filet mignon from now on." Gary smiled and squeezed Katelyn's hand that he was already holding in his.

"God, you're cheesy." She leaned over onto his right arm as Gary drove with his left hand. He felt her warmth seep into him. "Does that mean that if Miss America comes to town, I'm in trouble? Or any piece of filet mignon for that matter?" She smiled at Gary.

"Of course not. Look, I know it sounds weird, but I really do believe that there is someone out there for everyone. Just one person that we are supposed to end up with. Like I said before, I always looked at life as scripted. So why would I think that we were meant to have a bunch of chaos? I know that may sound odd, going through a divorce. But as hard of a time as I have had dealing with life being a larger improv act, I feel like eventually things are supposed to, well, ya know, be how they are supposed to be."

"You're just different," Katelyn added. "Most guys I meet in Klamath are drunk cowboys. Ya know, I once had a boyfriend make me feel like him cheating on me was my fault. And yes, she was off the dollar menu. He seemed to like the old rule that says you don't have to go for an 8-out-of-10 woman. You go for a 6 and drink until she is an 8." Katelyn paused and changed to a more serious tone. "I'm just not used to nice guys. And well, this sounds bad. But I never expected an attorney to be a good person."

"I know what you mean. But it's like there are two of me. There is attorney, and then there is person. For years, the person wasn't really allowed to be a person. I have to keep them separated to keep myself sane, but I slowly saw the attorney pouring into the person." Gary stared off down the road, seemingly away from the conversation. "Anyways, the attorney in me may not be a good person. I don't know. I don't feel like he is. But the person in me I think is."

"You said that you couldn't be you. But is it about who you are or who you want to be?" Katelyn inquired.

"Both. When it comes down to it, I did my own thing when I was with Staci. I still watched *Monday Night Raw*, *Star Trek*, and played video games. But I was made fun of. I guess I've always been used to getting made fun of on some level. So her criticism was normal from the beginning. It's about the freedom of not worrying about being made fun of. About feeling safe with who I am. About loving who I am. And I've hated myself for a long time. I still do. But now I feel like I can be who I want to be and learn to be okay with that."

"I get it. I just," Katelyn began. "I just don't get why you thought something was wrong with you."

"I'm twenty-nine years old, and I'm more excited about watching a Stone Cold stunner than having a drink with friends at a bar. I'm more excited about the prospect of a new *Star Trek* movie than some trendy Vin Diesel bullshit. I'm more excited about seeing bands that haven't released a hit album in two decades than singers who make new pop songs. To hell with Staci. Society has been telling me that there is plenty wrong with me for decades." Gary's face tensed, and he shook his head.

"And I'm twenty-two and supposed to be some stupid, backwoods, barefoot, in-the-kitchen, baby-making, Republican, man-pleasing hick. And until I met you, I started to buy into it. Joey made me feel like it was what I was too." Katelyn had a defeated look on her face.

"So how did you end that?" Gary asked.

"I guess I really didn't." Katelyn looked embarrassed. "I haven't called him since he got back from Pendleton."

"What's the plan then?" Gary asked while raising his eyebrows. He wasn't surprised that she hadn't told him, but he was hoping she had.

"No plan. Hopefully he just doesn't call me again and goes away."

Gary laughed. "That's what you do for a bill collector, not a fiancé."

"I know, I know," Katelyn began. "I don't want to hurt him, but I can't be with him. It's weird. I thought I was more of a hard ass than this."

"I get it. But if we are going to . . ." Gary started.

"Whatever this is, I'm not jeopardizing it," Katelyn assured Gary quickly. "I think I'll call him this weekend. He is going to be pissed. My sisters were both kind of teasing me about you one night.

He was drunk and, well, got really pissed. They were joking about you being cute. I kind of laughed it off, but Joey had a feeling that I was hiding something because of how I reacted."

"Are you going to tell him we got together?" Gary asked, part concerned, part amused.

"No, not yet. I don't think it is safe yet. And I don't want him to blow up on you. That is part of the problem. If I could tell him I've moved on, I don't think he would push it. If I don't tell him there is someone else, I don't think he will leave me alone." Katelyn pondered the issue, talking to herself, it seemed, as much as Gary.

"That's simple then," Gary said in an emphatic tone. "You tell him there is someone else and just don't tell him who."

"That might work. I should ask my mom for advice. She has broken more hearts in the last ten years than Madonna."

"Is that when your dad, well stepdad, went to prison?"

"Yes. It was weird. She kept telling us that she had been cheated on over and over again, but I'm not sure if I believe it. But since then, she has had guy after guy. She can't seem to be happy for more than a few months and sometimes has two or three guys chasing her at a time."

"That sounds fucking exhausting." Gary felt like he was worn out just thinking about it.

"Oh yes. And what really sucks is that my sister Carrie is just like her. The girl can't keep her mind on one cock for more than a couple hours."

"It's amazing that people continue to mimic their parents well after they are kids," Gary thought out loud.

"It's why Brandon can't be around all the drinking. It's why Sam can't be around the violence," Katelyn stated.

"Exactly." Gary nodded. "I miss him. I'm glad we are getting time together, but it is so hard to leave him."

"I know what you mean," Katelyn said. "I go through it every time I drop off Brandon. I thought it would get easier. But it almost gets harder."

Gary had stayed true to his word and allowed Staci to have Sam over the weekend so long as his mother-in-law was present and supervising the whole time. As such, Gary had called Katelyn, and they decided to have their first official date be out of town. Katelyn had thought that if they were in town, they couldn't do much, not that town had much to offer. They took off for Redding, California. Gary had mentioned he had visited there several times and had told her about a bridge with a giant sundial attached.

Amy had picked Sam up at about five thirty that night. It was bittersweet. Gary had anticipated his time with Katelyn all week. But giving up Sam was harder than he had imagined. The horror that he had worked so hard to prevent was coming alive. He didn't want a broken house for Sam. But here he was, having had to do a parenting time exchange. He knew that it was supervised. He knew that he was in the driver's seat for getting the majority of the time with Sam. He knew that he was not going to have to give Staci a lot of time soon. But even a day or two was too much.

The trip to Redding seemed to go by in seconds. It was as if Katelyn's company made time accelerate. They talked about everything from music, to movies, to books, to television, to food.

"What do you mean you don't like mustard?" Katelyn looked at him with exasperation.

"It's the devil's condiment. Tastes *horrible*," Gary replied.

"Not on hot dogs? Pretzels? What about deviled eggs?" Katelyn added.

"Ketchup on hot dogs. Cheese on pretzels. Mayonnaise only in deviled eggs," Gary replied.

"How do you live with all these rules? I only thought people in prison didn't eat mustard."

It was around 9:00 p.m. when they got into Redding. "Do you want to try to find a hotel room first and then go out?" Gary asked.

"And I thought you said you weren't like other guys." Katelyn smiled at him as she responded.

"Oh gosh, it's not like that. Well," Gary had to be honest. "Okay, it is sort of like that. At least, I'm unobjectionable to it. But I thought we might want to find someplace comfortable."

Gary found an economical hotel when they pulled into town. He opened the door to the hotel, and Katelyn followed him in. Gary had barely put his bag on the floor when Katelyn had jumped him. She kissed him with a fiery passion, the same passion she had back in his office. She slowly moved her mouth down to his neck, and Gary undid her belt. It was seamless. They were in sync on a level Gary could never have imagined. Without need for stimulation, he had slid into Katelyn and didn't move his lips from hers as they made love.

The same fire burned within him. He held her in his arms the entire time; their lips locked during the embrace. The mutual climax didn't end the embrace or the kissing; it only intensified it. This wasn't sex. It was something more. It was as if he really hadn't lost his virginity until that night in his office. Because whatever this was, it was better than sex. Making love was poetic. It was beautiful on a level he never thought possible.

Gary was scared of the prospect of ever losing this feeling. This new chapter of life was invigorating. The morose nature of the old chapter was stunning from this point of view. How could he have lived without this? He had only had Katelyn for one week. His lustful obsession was growing to love at a pace he could not comprehend.

"So this bridge," Katelyn asked as she pulled her boots back on. "I thought you said it was a sundial. Why are we going in the middle of the night?"

Gary smiled at Katelyn. Her hair was pulled from the hair tie in a way that could only happen during sex. "It's lit up from the bottom. It is a bridge you only walk on, no cars." They each put on their own clothes.

As they left the hotel room, Gary took Katelyn's hand in his. He walked her to the car door and let her in. Once in the car, Gary drove down toward the river that used the bridge as a crossing. Gary opened her car door when they parked. When they got out to walk toward the bridge, Gary took Katelyn's hand in his own. It felt natural. It felt right.

They walked hand in hand out onto the bridge. Smiling at each other but not talking much. It wasn't that they had exhausted topics of conversation, but as though they were comfortable enough with each other to simply enjoy the moment.

"Why me?" Katelyn had broken the silence as they stood in the middle of the bridge, looking over the river. "I'm not that smart, I'm not special, I don't get it. Your stupid filet mignon analogy is bullshit. Why would you pick me when I'm . . ." Katelyn hesitated, "plain?"

Gary stared out into the water and thought about how best to answer the question. "Just because people have told you that you aren't special or smart doesn't make it true. Your genuinely kind, beautiful, sexy, a good mother. I don't know what's not to like."

She smiled and tilted her head onto his shoulder. "I was wrong about you. You're an idiot." She chuckled.

Gary laughed loudly. "Why all the sudden am I an idiot?"

"Because every other guy who has ever looked at me has seen something different," Katelyn said with a depressed tone to her voice.

"They're the idiots." Gary turned his head to the right and kissed Katelyn on the top of the head.

"Well, ya, that's true," Gary felt her arms tighten around him.

"You kind of put yourself out there in a way I never thought anyone would," Katelyn added. "I mean, if this had gone bad for you, you could have really lost everything. And you risked that for me. I don't really know what to say." Gary saw tears began to build in Katelyn's eyes. He put his hands on her face and cleared the tears with his thumbs.

"You're right in a way. Yes, I barely know you. Quite frankly I've found out more about you in the last twenty-four hours than I did when I basically put my professional livelihood on the line. But since I can't let this go wrong now, I guess I have to put up with you not knowing who Led Zeppelin is."

"Okay, that isn't fair. You are super old compared to me." Katelyn's gloomy expression had turned to a large grin.

"Seven years apart does not make me super old. I think you just aren't cultured," Gary added as he pulled her in for a kiss.

"Me? Not cultured?" Katelyn exclaimed after they separated. "You are some super genius lawyer, and you have barely read Shakespeare." She rolled her eyes at him.

"That's not true, I read *Romeo and Juliet* and . . ." She glared at him as he lied through his teeth. "Okay, fine, I haven't read much of it. But in my defense he wasn't writing about an epic struggle between Harry Potter and He Who Must Not, which you have only watched, not read." It was Gary's turn to roll his eyes now.

"You are such a kid, how can you possibly compare the complex storylines created by Shakespeare with a children's book?"

"First of all, young-adult series. Second of all, Harry Potter deals with tons of serious topics: racism, bullying, poverty, death, child abuse, terrorism, political corruptness, and so much more," Gary named off the subjects with superior speed. "As for Shakespeare, his plays can often be reduced to simple storylines with limited complexity. *Hamlet*? It's *The Lion King* without Timon and Pumba. *Taming of the Shrew*? It's *10 Things I Hate about You* minus the awkward implications of high school."

"How many people do you have to justify that to? You seem to have that well-rehearsed. But you can't compare it to Shakespeare. Shakespeare has lasted the test of time better than any other piece of literature. Just because a storyline can be boiled down to its core to help a young audience appreciate it doesn't mean it isn't complex."

"Just because something is old doesn't make it better," Gary chimed in.

"That is sometimes true." Katelyn smiled at him. "But since you're the best man I've found, old it is."

CHAPTER 15

Love Is a Battlefield

It was a weekend that neither of them wanted to end. The ride back was much quieter than the ride there. The insecurities that they had brought with them had been extinguished. *Love* was a word that Gary didn't want to use yet. He had been officially separated from Staci for barely a week. True, he hadn't been in love in years. He hadn't said "I love you" . . . Well, he couldn't remember the last time. He knew he loved Katelyn. But when he had told Staci that he loved her, it was clunky. It was something that he said because the time had simply come to do so. But with Katelyn, it was different. It wasn't something gained over time. It was just there.

"So do we have to go back to this being a secret?" Katelyn began, "It's been so nice being able to just be us."

"Well, your case is practically done. We just need some signatures. But Joey still needs to know. And we should probably keep it private for a month or so. But I don't see any reason why we can't hang out with each other at home during the week and go out of town on the weekends," Gary answered and squeezed her hand little harder.

Gary felt his phone vibrate in his pocket. He pulled it out to see what was going on and noticed a text. It was Victoria Wampach. "Gary, I got a call from the sheriff just now, asking how to get a hold of you. He wanted me to give you his phone number to call him right away. I think it has to do with your son. They didn't know how to reach you, and since my husband works for the city, they had my number. Hope everything is okay. 541-530-8679."

Gary stared at the phone. Panic set in quickly, and he felt his heart throb. He pulled over to the side of the road. Katelyn looked over at Gary with concern. "Everything okay?" she asked, turning to him and placing her hand on his shoulder.

"I, um, I . . ." Gary had trouble getting the words out. "I don't know yet." He punched the numbers into his phone and called.

"Dispatch Operator."

"Hi, this is Gary Tornow. I was told by my friend Victoria Wampach to call. Something with my son?" Gary stumbled through the words.

"One second let me get a hold of the deputy," the operator began. "Okay, sir, your son is okay. Looks like they are holding your wife and son at the hospital here in Klamath Falls. She brought him there with some concerns, and the doctors couldn't figure out what she was saying, and they have some concern for your son's well-being and won't release her with him since they found the restraining order."

"Okay," Gary was still panicked. Whatever Sam had been through, Gary knew it must have been a crazy ride. How could Amy let them out of her sight? Gary shook his head in frustration. But he was over ninety minutes away. Panic flooded him again. "I'm out of town, a little under a couple of hours away."

"Since there is a restraining order, then your son won't be released until you arrive. I'll let the deputy on scene know."

"What going on?" Katelyn's face and voice were filled with anxiety.

"I don't really know still," Gary was thinking out loud. "She took him to the hospital. She must have shaken off her mom . . ."

"Or her mom doesn't think she is dangerous and let her do what she wanted." Katelyn's words were more harsh than anxious. Gary could sense Katelyn's anger toward Amy's incompetence.

"Probably, who knows? But he is safe. God knows what hell he has gone through though. I'll drop you off at home and then . . ."

"Drop me off at home? I want to be there for you for this," Katelyn told him.

It might have been the only thing that she could have possibly said that would have made Gary smile. "I know, and thank you for that. But not yet. People don't even know we are together yet, and they can't. After I get Sam back and see how he is, I'll give you a call, and you can come over if you want. I don't . . ." Gary hesitated, "I'm not exactly sure how I am going to be with being away from you."

Gary saw warmth run through Katelyn's cheeks. "Okay. I'll come over afterward, you're right. I need to deal with Joey anyways."

The rest of the drive was filled with anxiety. The thoughts of what Sam had been through in the short time Staci was unsupervised were flowing through his head. Was she smoking more than pot? What could she have said to him? What made her bring him to the hospital?

"So . . ." Katelyn's voice was filled with hesitation. "We talked about you being unhappy with Staci, but you never really talked about the insane things she has done. I mean, I know what happened most recently, but I mean, if you aren't ready . . ." Her voice trailed off.

Gary didn't answer immediately. He felt insecurity slowing seep back into him. Was he ready to tell her? What would she say about what he went through? Would she judge him for not leaving earlier? Gary turned his head toward her. His eyes met her eyes, and the security bled out of him again. He could trust her. He could always trust her.

"Well, we don't have enough time for everything, so let me start kind of at the beginning . . ."

Katelyn listened in silence as Gary walked her through a number of events. The time that Staci had punched a hole in the wall because Gary had shrunk her sweater in the washer, the time that Staci had thrown one of Gary's law school books out the window because she thought he was ignoring her, the time that Staci had thrown spaghetti at Gary because he had talked to another woman, and so on. He told her about Gary waking up to Staci singing to him, the suicide threats, the drug use, everything.

When Gary was done, Katelyn sat and took it in. "I get it," Katelyn said. It was the last thing Gary expected to hear.

"You get it?" Gary said, puzzled. "What part?"

"Why you didn't leave right away. Why you are leaving now, everything," Katelyn began. "I know what it means to be abused."

Gary hesitated. "You mentioned before that Donald, was it? Your stepdad, he had abused you?"

"Ya," Katelyn began, "but I don't know. I remember my uncle Bob. I remember him touching me, and I don't know why. It is like I blocked it out. But it keeps getting stronger and stronger."

"What is his last name?" Gary decided he needed to confirm his thoughts.

"Murray," Katelyn answered. "Do you know him?"

Gary paused. The answer "No" was his instinct. And he couldn't tell Katelyn anything that wasn't public. But Robert being a prominent businessman in town, the information had been published in the newspaper. Gary sighed. He picked up his phone, despite driving, and looked at the local news website and brought up the article on Robert's arraignment. "Yes, I do. And . . ." Gary paused. "I didn't know who he was before I took his case."

Katelyn's eyes bulged as she read, and Gary saw a small tear began to form in both of her eyes. "So he hurt someone else." It wasn't a question. "I don't know what to say. I . . ."

"I'm not defending what he did, obviously," Gary began.

"It's not your fault, it's your job," Katelyn reassured Gary. "But it is hard and is going to be hard on me. I want him dead, and it is your job to defend him."

"I'm sorry, I needed to be honest with you and . . ." Gary began but was interpreted by Katelyn squeezing tightly against his arm.

"It's okay. It is almost like you being with me is helping me break through things I blocked out. I just . . . I don't think . . ." Katelyn stumbled.

"What?" Gary squeezed her hand tightly.

"He doesn't deserve to live. Every time I have ever had sex with someone for the first time, it has been awkward and clunky, and it is because of him. Little things set me off, and I have flashbacks."

"Was our first time like that?" Gary asked in a serious and concerned tone.

"No, and that's just it. It's like it doesn't apply to you because I feel that I'm safe with you. No one has ever made me truly feel safe." Katelyn's warm eyes were looking up at his face again.

"Dead, huh?" Gary thought out loud.

"Dead," Katelyn affirmed. "I know it sounds terrible, but I wouldn't shed a tear if someone blew his head off. Maybe it would give me the closure I need. I don't know."

"Maybe. It's so final. It's hard to tell if it would help or make it worse," Gary told her.

"Honestly? I don't think that it would hurt anymore. Maybe that makes me a vengeful person, but even if it did make the flashbacks worse, knowing he was rotting would make it better." Katelyn gave a short laugh in order to hide the tears she was fighting back. "Look, today isn't about me anyway. Making sure Sam is safe is the important thing." Gary hadn't felt they were done tackling the subject but knew better than to push the issue. If she was ever ready to talk more, he would know.

"Fair enough," Gary told her and squeezed her again.

When they pulled into town, Katelyn gave Gary directions back to her house in a more efficient manner than he knew.

"Thank you for, well, everything," Gary told her as he took her bag from the back of his SUV.

"You don't have to thank me, I'm the one who gets to be thankful here." She smiled and leaned into him as he kissed her goodbye.

The lonely five-minute drive to the hospital may have lasted hours. He did not know what he was walking into. He didn't know what to expect. He grabbed a hoodie as he left the car and locked it, making his way to the emergency room.

"Excuse me," he asked a receptionist at triage. "Um, my son, Sam Tornow is here, and I . . ." The lady smiled at him and went to grab the door.

"This way, sir. The doctor wants to speak with you before you leave with your son." Gary nodded at her and walked through the door. She led him down the hall past the rooms that were covered in white curtains to a back family waiting room.

After Gary sat down, the nurse smiled at him, turned around, and closed the door behind her as she left. The room was cold and foreboding. This was not a room used to deliver good news. The seat he had taken was lumpy and uncomfortable. There were no windows in the room and no artwork on the walls.

A gentle knock came from the door. "Uh, um, come in," Gary said lightly. He found that his mouth had dried, and he had trouble forming words. This room seemed to magnify anxiety.

"Hi, uh, Mr. . . ." The doctor checked the notes in his hands. "Tornow? Tornow. Yes, um, I'm Dr. Stiles. Thank you for coming in." Dr. Stiles appeared to notice the look of anguish on Gary's face and quickly turned to a comforting tone. "I'll start by letting you know that your son is fine. Your wife—she told us you were separated—brought him in, saying that he had fallen out of bed in the middle of the night. We checked him and couldn't find anything wrong with him. He even told us he hadn't. Then she made accusations that he had been abused at his daycare. Again, we looked at him and found nothing."

"So," Gary interpreted as he began to think out loud, "I'm glad you called me because she isn't supposed to have unsupervised time with him, but um . . ." Gary gathered his thoughts, "it sounded like he was in some sort of danger?"

"Uh, well, you see, we really can't tell. Staci, your wife, has been acting incredibly strange. Because of this, one of the nurses looked up her records and found that she had recently been at Phoenix House and had a strict medicine regime she was supposed to stick to. But it looks like she never picked up the medicine from the pharmacy. At first, my impression was that she was under the influence of methamphetamines. She was itching, very frantic, incoherent, loud, and very difficult to keep on topic." The doctor closed his notes and looked up as if he expected Gary to comment.

Gary shook his head to clear it. "None of it surprises me. Her mom was supposed to be with her. Have you seen her?" Gary inquired.

"No, just her. One of the officers that responded to my call earlier I guess looked up a restraining order and saw who she was supposed to be with. I don't remember the name though."

"Okay." Gary nodded. "Can Sam and I leave now?"

"I have some paperwork for you. Someone from the Department of Human Services was here earlier." The doctor handed him a card. "She asked that you call her in the morning to talk about what happened here."

Gary thought to himself for a moment and then decided to press the issue. "What do you think is wrong with her? Phoenix House seemed to think that she was self-medicating for depression with drugs. You make it sound like there is something else."

"Well, she isn't really my patient, so I don't know," Dr. Stiles answered sheepishly, seeming to decide if he should answer further. "But she seems to suffer from some form of manic depression. A lot of people are diagnosed with it that shouldn't be. But she definitely has the symptoms. She has a lot of extreme ups and down. Medicine can effectively treat it, but the issues with it are circular. People who have it don't like to take the medicine because they are often paranoid about it. And when they do take the medicine, they often stop after it really starts to take effect and then fall back into cycles." Then he paused for a few moments. "But again, I don't really know. I'm not treating her. Just observing the impact she is having on your guys' son."

"Thank you, Doctor. Can I see him now?"

"Sure. We have him in a kids' room the hospital typically reserves for observing abused kids, but it is because we don't have a lot of places to keep kids at when they aren't really sick." Dr. Stiles smiled for the first time and opened the door for him.

The room he was led to was full of much more life, and as Gary saw the back of Sam, he seemed to breathe fully for the first time in hours. "Sam," Gary called at him. Sam turned around in the chair and smiled. He was holding a blue crayon, apparently drawing at the table he was seated at.

"Daddy!" Sam ran over to him and hugged him around the waist. "I drew you a picture." Sam pointed to the table. Gary held his hand and walked over to it. Some of it he could make out. It kind of looked like a whale, a monkey, and some sort of dinosaur.

"Very cool, Sam," Gary told him, and he bent over and hugged him. Gary noticed Dr. Stiles standing in the doorway. Gary thought it was a good opportunity to try to get Sam to talk with a witness. "Sam, so where was your grandma at? I thought she was going to be with you guys?"

"I don't really know. Grammy was there, and then she went outside, and Mommy said we had to go, so we got in the car without Grammy." Sam had turned his attention back to the drawing as he grabbed another crayon.

Gary grabbed his phone out of his pocket and scrolled through is contacts to Amy's name. He wrote her the text message "What the hell happened?" hoping she would respond, and he could figure out more of what had gone on.

"Sam, let's head home, okay, buddy?" Gary asked.

Sam nodded at him and grabbed his hand. He picked up the picture he had colored in his other hand. As they began to leave, a sheriff appeared at the door. "Actually, Sam, go ahead and go back and color for a moment. I have to talk to the police officer, okay?" Sam nodded again.

"John, nice to see a friendly face." Gary had recognized the sheriff from his various dealings with law enforcement on cases.

"Gary." The sheriff tipped his hat. "We don't see each other outside of work so often. Sorry it is in these circumstances. So you know it is a mandatory arrest for her restraining order violation. Sounds like she is nuts, so I don't think anything else will come out of it, but she will probably be released tomorrow. I just want to make sure you guys have some place safe you can stay."

"Ya, um," Gary thought, "I really don't see her coming by the house."

"Do you have protection?" John asked.

Gary didn't think he was talking about condoms. "No, um, I don't own a gun, if that's what you mean."

"Jeez, with all those wackos you represent, I would think you would have gotten one by now. Look, it may not be my place, but maybe you should consider getting one," John said with a small chuckle.

Gary responded without words and nodded.

CHAPTER 16

● ● ● ● ● ● ●

Boundaries

It seemed that the principles Gary had kept close to him for a number of years were disappearing daily basis. Marriage vows? For better or worse, for sickness and in health . . . it never mentioned what the hell you do if your spouse turns into a crazy drug addict. Boundaries with clients? Having just gotten back from a weekend of copulation with Katelyn, he could easily say that he had not only blurred the line but had completely rid himself of it. Two new principles now presented themselves for demolition.

Gary looked over at the contents in the passenger seat of his car. At the sheriff's advice, Gary had gone out and purchased a small handgun and a lock box to store it in. Up until now, Gary's view on having a gun in the home was twofold. First, Gary thought about the true reason he had never gotten one. The reason for the majority of the relationship with Staci was that he thought that he would come home to Staci in the kitchen having blown her own head off. Later on, Gary was afraid he would wake up to the barrel of gun in his eyes. But truly, Gary had never been comfortable with guns. He had nothing against owners of guns, in general at least, but they were not for him. They always made him nervous. Gary had never been a violent person, and somehow, purchasing the gun knowing that the one and only reason he would ever use it would be to defend himself from Staci made him feel like he had crossed the line and had somehow agreed that violence was a viable solution. But was there another solution if it came down to it? No, not likely. It didn't make it any easier to accept the change.

The other principle which had been a cornerstone of his career that he faced today was objectivity. Gary had built success by being able to separate his emotion from every case he had ever handled. Even with Katelyn, Gary's advice to her was solid. It was hard to give her objectivity when he had wanted to win for her, but nonetheless, he was able to.

But now a new challenge presented itself. Gary had checked his calendar on his phone when he woke up. His first appointment, with Eddie Gutierrez, showed how he could still be objective. No doubt that Eddie was a terrible person. However, Gary could separate the actions of the man from the rights that the law granted him. However, it was his late appointment that brought him turmoil.

Robert Murray was Katelyn's uncle. The crimes that he was accused of were not against Katelyn, but Gary knew that Robert had hurt her. Gary had negotiated Robert a plea bargain that he thought was a steal. Robert would be allowed to plead to a misdemeanor and face no jail time, just probation and sex offender registration. Somehow, the win felt shallow. He had taken a client who faced prison and negotiated a deal to where the man would not face another day in jail.

Someone not involved in the law might look at the idea of pleading to a crime in any way a loss. But the truth was that most cases ended in a plea deal. But most of the time the end result was somewhat proportionate to the crime. The accusations in this case, however meager, still involved heavy charges. Getting to walk away with your liberty was rare for those charged with sex abuse, and Robert Murray would have that option.

Gary's inner turmoil pulled him in multiple directions. He had never been a violent man, but the struggles with Staci had erupted a beast inside him, which seemed to thirst for it. It fed on the very thought of taking his pain and the pain of those he loved and converting it to vengeance. He had never been in a proper fight before and had no clue what striking another felt like. Years ago, he had a girlfriend in high school who, instead of just breaking up with him, had made out with a guy at a party. It was the only other time Gary had truly felt a pull toward vengeance and violence. Even then, he did not fight his own battles. He had allowed, well persuaded actually, a friend to provoke the guy who stolen his girlfriend into a fight in the hallway. The guy ended up with a bloody nose, his friend suspended, and Gary walked away feeling awful about himself but unbloodied and unpunished.

When Gary had arrived and looked in his office, the first thing he noticed was his in-tray. It was on par with the kind of chaos that was in his life and was a reflection of how his personal life had created chaos for him in his professional life. Gary had known for years the devastation that divorce had on someone's life, no matter how long the marriage had been their life. Change creates chaos in and of itself. Gary sighed, double-checked his calendar, and then began to dig into the in tray.

After about an hour of steady work, Gary felt rather accomplished. Big projects and cases were not what had been neglected but little things such as short letters to clients and reviewing some reports and plea offers. Gary's anxiety had been lowered exponentially by getting through some of the work. He looked up and realized that Eddie would be in the office within five minutes. He cleared his desk and pulled out the file.

Eddie's case had been dismissed several days before in a rather anticlimactic fashion. With the motion to suppress being successful, the Department of Justice was left with no more evidence and had to concede defeat. Gary had called Eddie to tell him the good news, and Eddie's response, while a happy one, lacked the enthusiasm that Gary had expected after getting Eddie out of a possible twenty-year prison sentence. Gary was surprised when he had gotten a call that Eddie wanted to come in person to meet with him.

"Gary, Mr. Gutierrez is here to see you," Marti had appeared at the door.

"Ya, um, send him in," Gary was still in his thoughts when Marti had appeared.

"Mr. Tornow, it is a pleasure to see you again." Gary noted that Eddie's wife was not with him. She had been with him at every turn. Either they had a falling out due to the chaos of all that had happened or he had something to discuss that his wife was not to know about.

"Eddie, it is nice to see you as well," Gary responded. "So your case has been dismissed, and I've submitted paperwork for the arrest to be expunged. Since you weren't convicted, we are allowed to do so right away. There isn't much more to do on your case—"

"Well, I wanted to talk about something else." Gary was interrupted. "We still have confidence, yes?" Eddie asked.

Gary thought for a moment, trying to figure out what Eddie was referring to, and Gary went back to his original thoughts, which were that somehow this meeting was not connected to the case. "Oh, you mean our conversations are still confidential?" Eddie nodded to Gary's words. "Yes, yes, of course, what's on your mind?"

"Look, you're a very smart man. One of the smartest I've ever met. You know who I work for." It wasn't a question; it was a statement. Gary didn't say anything. There was no need to confirm what they both knew. "Well, I have kids, I have a wife. Nobody wants to hire me to do honest work unless it is mucking stalls. I'm not a bad man, but I am who I have to be for my family."

"What happened?" Gary asked.

"I saw something," Eddie began.

"Just saw?" Gary questioned.

"No, not just saw." Eddie paused for several moments after answering as if he was either second-guessing coming here or he was truly afraid of what he was about to say. "I'm afraid because one of my friends, Jose Plancarte, got arrested last night. He was there, and I don't know what he has said to anyone." Eddie hesitated again. "Most of the time, people owe money or something for drugs, prostitutes, gambling, whatever, I rough them up. I might break a thumb, the old-fashioned thing to do. I might bruise ribs, it just depends. Mostly, I don't hurt anyone in a way they can't recover. Our business needs them to work in order to pay us back. But one night, Jose went a little too far." Eddie had paused and looked like he needed encouragement to continue.

"It's okay, go on, tell me," Gary reassured him.

"We have a way that we always do things. The boss wasn't sure how many people or if any would be with the guy, so he sent two of us. Usually, I ask the guy to confess his sins. I show up, toss him around a little bit, then make him get on his knees and pray. I tell him to confess his sins. Then if he needs some guidance to remember what he did, I tell him generally, like he stole something or didn't pay a debt. I make them tell me why I'm there. For some reason, Mr. Gr—" Eddie began before correcting himself, "The boss, he thinks that them confessing makes it more likely that they will pay up. Doing it on your knees before God."

"What happened?"

"He wouldn't confess. All he said to us was 'You fuckers are going to prison. I ain't talking and everyone knows you don't kill anyone, just rough them up. Well, rough me up. I know your faces. Let me go now, and maybe I'll forget.' Jose didn't like that. We carry guns not because we want to kill the customers but intimidate them. The guy laughed. Jose was in front of him with the gun to his forehead. The guy was crazy, he just laughed. Then Jose pistol-whipped him, looked like he broke his jaw. He wasn't laughing anymore. He started yelling, saying that he hoped we had families so that people we loved would have to see what pieces of shit we were. That our children would watch us go to prison. Then . . ." Eddie had paused, not wanting to finish.

"You shot him because the idea of you going to prison and leaving your family terrified you," Gary finished. Eddie nodded affirmatively.

"We were at the guy's house, and I flew his brains all over the living room. Jose laughed; he said that it's the last time we will ever have to worry about someone saying that we never kill anyone. We cleaned the house and used ammonia to dilute the blood. We wiped off everything we had touched. We wrapped the body in some garbage bags and threw it in the back of Jose's truck. We drove halfway to Reno and buried him about five hundred feet off a highway."

"Is anyone going to miss this guy?"

"He was a junkie, but he worked at the window-and-door factory. They probably noticed when he didn't show up. But he seemed to be a loner. They might just think he skipped town."

"Look, I don't know what Jose is going to say, but I don't think that he is going to confess that," Gary tried to reassure him. "Unless they have evidence, and I don't even think that a crime of this nature has been in the news recently. It's more likely that Jose got picked up for his other involvement."

"But couldn't he sell me out for a better deal?" Eddie asked.

"If someone in your, well, 'occupation,' sells somebody out, do they live long?" Gary asked, almost rhetorically.

"That's true." Eddie nodded, staring at the desk in front of him.

"Look, if it comes to be, we will do what we can to combat it. But it happened, and you are going to have to live with the fact that this could come back to haunt you at any time. There is no statute of limitations. You can only hope the case goes cold with no leads. But the fact that the Department of Justice has taken such an interest in your organization tells me that you might be in for a scuffle."

"I can't flee. I have to stay here and try to fight. I'd rather die in prison having used a chance to stay with my family than run and never see them again, not knowing what would have happened."

"We don't know what is happening yet, just be calm. Either way, last time something happened, Mr. Greenburg bought you a good defense. Perhaps he can do the same again. We will do what we can. A charge like murder, though, I can do a lot of miracle work, but I'm not going to lie to you, if you get charged, it's going to be an uphill battle," Gary wanted to be honest about the situation with Eddie.

"I don't think Mr. Greenburg paying is an option," Eddie answered.

"Why is that?" Gary inquired.

"The guy we killed owed him over $10,000. He takes the fact that I killed him, and he can no longer collect very seriously. He was reluctant to pay for my last defense but said it was like throwing money at bad money. That I had already cost him $10,000 and that I was proving to be a bad investment. That getting arrest, killing someone I was just supposed to rough up, it was too dangerous for him and that I was on my own if I screwed up again."

Gary felt for Eddie in many ways. He understood why Eddie was who he was. And he felt compelled to help him. "I can't work for free, but hopefully, we can work something out if it comes to it. I'll think of something. Maybe I have some work you can do in exchange for services or something."

"Thank you, Mr. Tornow. You've already saved my family once, and I don't know how to thank you enough."

"Well, like I said, we'll figure that out." Gary smiled.

After Eddie left, Gary searched newspaper records, online reports, and even his e-mails for any sign of a murder similar to the one Eddie had described. Nothing. He also looked at Jose Plancarte's charges. Two counts of racketeering. No murder charges. So far so good.

"Gary, Mr. Murray is here to see you." Marti had appeared again. He thought that he had over an hour until Robert was to arrive, but looking at the clock, he realized he had spent much more time than he had expected searching for issues that might come into play with Eddie.

Marti led Robert into his office. "Robert, come in, sit down, I have good news," Gary greeted him as Marti shut the door behind her. The sight of Robert ignited Gary. It burned images into his head of what Katelyn must have gone through. He felt like lunging at him. Like strangling him. Gary restrained himself.

"Okay," Robert responded. He seemed to be very anxious and a bit agitated.

"Everything all right?"

"Just nervous," Robert answered.

"Well, I have news that might help. I have negotiated a deal for you. In it, you would plead to sex abuse 2, reduced to a misdemeanor. You wouldn't face any additional prison or jail time. You would have a fine of $2,500, which would have to be paid off by the end of your probation period, which would be three years. Also, you would have to pay out of pocket for counseling for the victim."

"So I'd have to plead guilty?" Robert asked.

"I might be able to get them to stipulate to no contest, but I don't think so. Part of this is accepting culpability for your crime." Gary noticed in his own tone he was being harsher than he normally would be with a client and made an effort to correct it, despite the fact that he wanted to castrate Robert. "The fact is that they have enough evidence that they might be able to convince a jury. Juries like to convict in these cases. And if they did so in this case, you are looking at least six years in the state penitentiary. Guilty, not guilty, it protects your liberty."

"Would I have to register as a sex offender?" Robert inquired. He still looked nervous.

"Yes," Gary answered swiftly, again with the harsh tone.

"What does that entail?" The tone of Robert's voice did not match Gary's harshness. It was a tone of concern, of caution.

"You register every year, usually within ten days of your birthday, with the county. After about ten years, we might be able to get the registration status removed. But you provide them with your address and an update on your appearance. You will have to complete a sex offender program in order to be able to be around kids again. In that, you talk about what happened in your case. They also ask about past victims, etc." Gary threw in the past victims part unconsciously. He knew that he wanted to know more but in the same breath thought he knew too much.

"Past victims?" Robert asked. There was hesitation and concern in his voice.

The question stoked the vengeful fires that had awoken inside of Gary. It was clear to Gary that Robert would never take responsibility for the actions against Katelyn. Gary was not sure if that was what he wanted though. Did he need Robert to confess? Did he need the satisfaction of him saying what he did to Katelyn? Did he need him to say sorry? Did it matter how Robert felt about it at all?

Gary realized he paused for an abnormal amount of time and shook his head vigorously to snap out of his destructive train of though.

"Robert, we have met enough times, and I have read enough information to tell that something is going on here. Maybe not with this particular crime. But"—Gary both felt the need to be harsh as a professional and on a personal level—"the truth is that your family seemed to anticipate this. They seemed to take issue with your behavior for a long time. Perhaps, this crime in this manner of punishment helps you avoid getting pinched later on for something else if you get help."

"I don't, I don't want help. I don't need help . . . I . . ." Robert began to sob violently into his hands.

Others needed help, not him. Others deserved help, not him. And Gary was here offering him help nonetheless. He was offering him a path to redemption on a silver platter, yet Robert stood defiant, continuing to deny the issues in front of them.

"The deal is only good for a few more days," Gary responded to the tears in flat voice. He pushed the box of tissues unceremoniously toward Robert. "I need to know what you want to do. Do you want to take it?"

Robert continued to sob but responded by nodding affirmatively. "Why is this happening? I feel like I'm a good person. And now I have to register as a sex offender? I never thought this could happen to me, I never thought . . ."

"Robert, with all due respect," Gary interrupted with the common phrase used only before moments of disrespect, "the actions you have taken during your lifetime have lead you to this place. It may not be that this incident itself was bad, but you hesitated when I mentioned past victims."

"I . . . I don't know what you mean," Robert said the words in a flat tone, trying to hide his concern and revealing he knew exactly what Gary meant.

"You don't have your own kids, but you have relatives, right?" Gary asked the question in a rhetorical manner, already knowing the answer, of course. "You take this deal and the likelihood of getting charged for anything that happened with them is low." Gary felt like a sword had pierced his stomach. Never would Robert truly face justice, and Gary was providing him with the vessel. Gary felt like it was time to push the issue and make Robert understand the sweetness of the deal. "Robert, I have met too many people that have been charged with this crime and looked at too many people's reactions when I ask them about past victims or guilt for the crime that they have been charged with. I don't know who else you have hurt, but I can tell there is a past involved here. You need to get better, or the next time this happens, you could end up in prison or killed by an angry dad, mom, or boyfriend," Gary added the boyfriend remark, thinking of curb-stomping Robert's sheepish look off his face. The violent beast within Gary had reached a boiling point. How? He was not violent. He was not impulsive. He was not a monster. Not, he wasn't a monster, but before him a monster sat. Someone whom those vengeful thoughts could not turn away from.

"I know that, I know . . ." There was hesitation in Robert's voice. "I know that I haven't been perfect, but I've never hurt anyone on purpose. I . . ."

"I'll let the district attorney know that you'll accept the offer. We will set up a plea date and . . ."

"No, no, I . . . I . . . I . . . I can't do it." Robert turned around. "I can't admit to this. My wife is already on the verge of leaving me. I can't do it. My life is ruined, prison or no prison, if I'm convicted. I have to . . ." Robert hesitated. "I guess I have to go to trial." Robert looked at the floor. "Win, lose, or draw, I need you to take this to trial. Can we win?"

"Yes," Gary said flatly. "I don't know if we will win or not, but we can. Juries like to convict on these kind of charge. But yes. It means that you owe me another $25,000. I need that ASAP."

"I can do that today." Robert sniffled. "I gotta do it. I don't have a choice in this."

"Okay then. Marti will take the fee outside. I'll let the district attorney know, and we will get ready to plan the trial."

"Thank you, thank you, Gary. It means a lot. All of your work does." It made him nauseas to think about the work he had put in. And now it was a possibility of him walking with no punishment. It felt wrong not only for Katelyn but for everyone else that he might have hurt.

Gary just nodded. He didn't want Robert to be thankful for his work. He wanted him to face justice. To pay for his sins. He wanted him to bleed for what he had done. Gary felt like he hardly knew himself anymore. He wanted this man to pay for the pain he had caused Katelyn. Fuck the twisted sense of needing to defend this person's rights. It all felt wrong, even more sick and sadistic than it ever had before.

"I'm heading out, you need anything?" Marti had appeared at his door as soon as he had heard the front door to the office close behind Robert. Apparently, the payment went through without issue. A payment for money that for the first time in Gary's life felt dirty. He felt cheap and used taking it.

"No, I'll see you in the morning," Gary answered flatly, still with his thoughts. Marti had already gathered her things and had pelted for the front door. She must have been running late. He heard the lock of the door click behind her.

Gary sat and pondered what he was going to do for several minutes. He tried to calm his thoughts and stay his emotions. Nothing worked. Robert had looked at the angry fire within Gary that yearned for vengeance, for justice, for blood, and had done nothing to put it out. He poured gasoline onto that monster, and it grew into something that he could no longer cage. Then taking a deep breath, he slowly picked up the phone.

"Eddie? Gary Tornow here. Can you come by my office tonight? I have a proposition for you in terms of payment for future services."

CHAPTER 17

● ● ● ● ● ● ●

Emiliiiiiiiiiiiiiooooooooooooooooooooooo!

The meeting was very brief. "I just want justice, not anything outrageous and not something you haven't done before. Rough him up, do your whole routine. Just make sure it doesn't get traced back to you and especially not back to me. Don't kill him, I don't want that. I just . . . he hurt somebody I care about, and he isn't going to pay for it in any other way."

Eddie was silent most of the meeting. He nodded a lot. At the end, he smiled widely and said, "I'll take care of it. I guess the things they say about lawyers are true, huh?"

Were they true? Gary wasn't sure which part he was referring to. The stereotype he had always heard fell in line with the persona he had to assume whenever he represented a criminal defendant. Looking past justice to the money. But now, he was looking past the money for justice. It wasn't right. But the image of Robert molesting Katelyn played through his mind and ate at it like acid. Gary didn't know if in the end it would help or not. But the look on Robert's face when Gary had mentioned past victims was burnt into Gary's eyes. Justice must be done.

The risk seemed minimal for some reason when he had made the call to Eddie, but now sitting at home on the couch with Katelyn leaning back against him and his arms tight around her the risk seemed astronomical. When he had made the phone call, he only thought of justice. He didn't think about the risks he was taking. About the people that could be hurting if this got fucked up. About Sam. About Katelyn. He had thought about Katelyn sure and about someone like Robert Murray living in the same town as Sam going unchecked, but not in the sense of what would happened if he was subtracted from their lives.

"Are you sure that you are okay? You seem distracted," Katelyn had noticed Gary staring off.

"No, I'm fine. Sorry, long day," Gary replied, trying to be casual.

Sam had gone to bed around eight, and Gary invited Katelyn over. It was still too early to introduce Sam to Katelyn. Not because he didn't believe that Katelyn and him had something so powerful that it wouldn't last but because Gary didn't want Sam to hold the divorce against Katelyn. He wanted to give Sam some time to adjust first before throwing his newfound love at him.

Gary had ordered a pizza, trying to keep things simple. They still didn't feel comfortable going out at night.

"How was it? The world of being an attorney has to be exciting every day, right?" Katelyn asked, somewhat rhetorically.

Gary sighed. "Sometimes it is too exciting," he replied. "It's hard to concentrate with everything going on around me. I bought that gun this morning, like I told you I would. It feels weird. And then . . ." Gary tried to sound casual again as he didn't want to approach the subject of Robert Murray. "Well, I had to deal with some clients that aren't a lot of fun. But it's okay."

The look on Katelyn's face told Gary that he had failed. "I don't know how you do it," Katelyn said somewhat sharply. The look on her face softened almost immediately after she said it. She must have realized that her words cracked like a whip. "I mean, you are such a good person and you have to deal with scumbags. I don't know how you don't just let some of them go to prison instead of helping them."

"Part of me wants to. Every time it does. But I think about the future the money means for Sam. I think about the fact that although I hate helping them get away that ultimately it creates a system where I don't have to worry about the police knocking down my door and dragging me away for no reason," Gary finished his glass of wine in a final chug. Katelyn seemed to notice that as well but seemed to choose to ignore it, already determining that something was wrong with Gary's demeanor.

"You really think that could happen?" Katelyn drank the final swig of her wine as well and poured both of them another, apparently resigning herself to the fact that they would be drinking.

"It has happened at every turn in history when a country's prevailing emotion has been fear. A lot of times, I feel like our country is on the brink of that. Our justice system keeps us in check." Gary had almost finished another glass of wine.

"Is there ever going to be a night when you come home and we don't have an in-depth conversation about the world and life and just chill out?" Katelyn's question seemed serious, but her tone showed amusement.

"Probably not." Gary chuckled as he responded. "Sounds fucking boring without it."

Katelyn and Gary had talked extensively about what movie to watch together. They came to the conclusion that they should each pick a movie but that they would do it under certain guidelines to make it kind of fun and to get to know each other. They decided that what they would do is each pick an actor or actress that they really liked. Katelyn would go first. Then the other would have to pick another actor or actress that played in at least one movie with the first one. Then the person who picked first would have to pick a movie with those to actors or actresses in it.

Katelyn, going first, picked Emilio Estevez. Gary had picked Molly Ringwald. Katelyn, not knowing Molly Ringwald, did a quick internet search, and they landed on *The Breakfast Club*. After they picked the movie, part of the game that helped them get to know each other was explaining each of your choices to the other person. Katelyn had picked Emilio Estevez, hoping as one of her favorites movies as a kid was *The Mighty Ducks*. Gary admitted it was the first thing he thought of when he thought of Emilio Estevez but that he couldn't remember anyone else in the movies. Gary picked Molly Ringwald because Katelyn had mentioned she never saw most of the truly iconic movies from the eighties.

"Okay, you said this was special. And it was pretty cool, don't get me wrong, but isn't every teen-coming-of-age bullshit movie basically the exact same thing?" Katelyn remarked after the movie ended.

"All of them *after* this one," Gary answered. "It's the first time Hollywood took the emotions of teenagers and saw them as complex and important."

"I really enjoyed it, but you realize they only considered the emotions as complex and important, as you put it, because it profits them?" Katelyn was smiling but made a good point.

"That's true and probably right about every movie that followed in its footsteps, but the first one of its kind, like most things first of their kind, you don't know how they will do in terms of sales. You don't know until you put your art out there." Gary looked down at Katelyn with glowing warmth and reached around, kissing her right cheek and strengthening his embrace.

"I guess that makes sense. It's your turn to choose, if you want to call it that, considering you basically had me choose off a list with one movie." Katelyn smirked and wrapped her arms tighter around Gary's arms.

With his pick of the movie, Gary picked his favorite comedian growing up, Mike Myers. Katelyn also picked Mike Meyers. "So what you are saying is that I have to pick a movie where Mike Myers plays at least two roles, right?"

"Yeah, baby!" Katelyn exclaimed.

"Hmm, well, if the point of this is so we get to know each other, I've already found out that we both like *Austin Powers*, so I don't need to go there. Let's do *So I Married an Axe Murderer*."

"He plays multiple people in more than one movie?" Katelyn asked with a surprised tone.

"Yes, it's an awesome movie. He plays the main character and the main character's dad. You'll never be able to listen to the song 'If You Want My Body' with a straight face again," Gary said excitedly.

"I don't think I listened to it with a straight face before." Katelyn rolled her eyes but smiled nonetheless. "I think that you designed this game so that somehow you get to pick every movie." Katelyn had a fake grimace move across her face.

"Oh, come on, Emilio Estevez has like four movies he is known for, three of which are Mighty Ducks movies. You picked a list with four movies on it, not me." Gary giggled.

"Uh-huh," Katelyn said sarcastically. "Then you somehow get yourself out of picking *Austin Powers* when I had you in a corner."

"Oh, come on, you loved it," Gary stated.

"Hardly the point," Katelyn answered with a smile. "I like the game, but tomorrow night, I'm picking the movies straight up. I think I'll go with something girly and . . ."

Gary had kissed her at that moment as she leaned back, cupping her left cheek in his left hand as he did so, holding her in place. Their lips embraced for what seemed like years, but it was likely only a brief moment.

"Don't think you got out of *The Notebook* tomorrow." Katelyn laughed after unlocking he kiss. Gary chuckled, and it was Katelyn's turn to kiss him, turning her body and straddling him.

Gary picked Katelyn up, and she wrapped her legs more tightly around him. He carried her to the bedroom, and without breaking their kiss, Katelyn flicked off the lights in the living room.

Gary saw the sun shine brightly through the curtains, piercing his eyes.

"Daddy, I want chocolate milk," he heard the voice say softly to him.

Gary looked behind him and saw Sam staring at him, holding out a cup.

"Okay, little buddy." Gary had made to get up but then realized his arm was trapped under Katelyn, who was wearing nothing but one of his old T-shirts.

"Who's that?" Sam asked.

"What?" Katelyn asked with a groggy shake and a stretch. Quickly realizing Sam was in the room, she pulled the blankets up over her bare bottom half. "Hi, Sam."

"Hi. What's your name?" Sam asked.

"Katelyn," she said with a frog in her throat.

"Wait, are you Brandon's mommy? Daddy, is she Brandon's mommy?" Sam asked excitedly as he looked between the two of them.

"Yes, buddy, that is Brandon's mommy." Only the truth would really work here he thought. "Buddy, go to the kitchen, I'll grab that milk for you."

Sam left the room. Gary made to get up and realized that he was also naked . . . and apparently erect. He grabbed his boxers quickly off the ground.

"That went smoothly," Gary added as he finally stood up.

The look on Katelyn's face was a mixture of horror and laughter. "You realize," Katelyn began to whisper quietly, "that although I technically have been introduced to him before, the first image that your son will have of us together will be both our bare asses pointed at him as he asked for a sugary dairy product?" Her beauty was breathtaking. With her hair unkempt and her shirt wrinkled from being on the floor most of the night, she was the most beautiful thing in the world to Gary.

Katelyn's words played through Gary's head for a moment. "Ugh. Maybe I should get some sort of installment plan with a child therapist, pay them in advance for how screwed up this situation may make him."

"Mostly his mom's fault, but if he heard us last night, I'm sure we ran the bill up." Katelyn was dressed now. She kissed him on the cheek as she made to leave the room. "Guess it is time to just go all in, let's get breakfast going."

CHAPTER 18

Drawing Dead

One of his biggest fears was quickly turning out to be false. Sam needed a mother. Gary knew that Staci would eventually wiggle her way back into Sam's life even if it was for a small amount of time every other weekend. But for now, Katelyn was filling the role in spectacular fashion. Baking cookies with him, helping with Legos, getting him dressed for bed. Nothing out of the ordinary, but it was a great change. Gary knew that Katelyn understood how important Sam was to him. Very quickly, Brandon and Sam began to bond and they quickly became a small family within days. Everything seemed to be moving at warp speed. Katelyn was spending most nights at Gary's house. When Katelyn had Brandon, she would spend the night at her own home, but they would be at Gary's late, often until the boys were on the verge of sleep.

Work was becoming more and more complicated. Gary found himself with a heavy disdain for his entire caseload. Rapists, burglars, people trying to get a divorce, it all sickened him. He hadn't neglected his work per se, but he hadn't been himself. He knew his waxing and waning interest was normal. He saw plenty of people go through divorces that had trouble adjusting personally. The chaos from the divorce, coupled with the extreme amount of time and attention he was dedicating toward Katelyn left little time for him to hang around his office.

Gary knew that eventually he would regret not going to professional engagements during this time period, and he knew that eventually Katelyn would want him to put some concentration back on his career for all of their sakes. So when Gary saw an invitation to a charity poker tournament for all the lawyers in town hosted by the local bar association, Gary RSVP'd right away. He asked Marti if she could watch Sam that night and texted Katelyn about the event.

"I have a poker tournament I want to go to tonight. Is that okay?" Gary had texted.

"No, you only get to spend time with me," she first sent, and then, "JK, you need to do it, sweetie. Besides, my family is starting to wonder if I'm dead. I'll call my sisters and have a girls' night."

He wasn't sure what kind of reaction he would get from the other attorneys. He knew Victoria and Adam would be there. They never turned down an occasion to drink. He was hoping to see a couple of his friends that he only saw on rare occasions. There were maybe a couple dozen attorneys in town; just enough would show up to occupy one poker table.

"Hey, dude, come on in." Peter Ashen, one of the older attorneys in town, answered the door. A lot of these parties seemed to take place at his house. Peter in his mid-sixties with long gray hair. He was short and now wearing a Hawaiian shirt and smelled like a mixture of bourbon and weed.

"Thanks, Peter, glad to see you." Gary shook his hand. Peter shook it more violently than he normally would have, appearing to have started the party early.

"Cool, man, glad to see you, glad to see you. Hey, man, look, sorry about what you are going through. I damn near died going through my two divorces. Anyways, everyone is back here. Grab a brew on your way in." Gary followed Peter down the hallway to a small room with dim lighting. In the middle sat a large poker table. Adam and Victoria were there. So were Brittany Tanner, Alanis Link, Preston Lee, and a couple of younger attorneys he recognized but didn't know on a first name basis.

"Gary is here everyone. Gary, you know everyone, right?" Peter looked back at him.

Gary made eye contact with the two he didn't know. "Gary Tornow," he said once, shaking their hands in turn.

"Oliver."

"Janice."

"Awesome. Well, no one else RSVP'd, so I guess just the seven of us. This is for charity. Fifty bucks a piece, half to the food bank, half to winner. Throw it in, ladies." Everyone took out the money and threw it in a hat that Peter was now holding out.

It was a nice change of pace. Everyone took turns dealing. "So, Gary," Peter asked, "going through his divorce, you seeing anybody?"

"Eh, not really," Gary answered quickly as he took a drink of beer. "I just don't have the time."

Adam Rose looked up from a pair of cards he apparently didn't like as he threw them in the middle of the table with disgust. "Dude, I have been married for seven years, and don't get me wrong, I love her, but man, I miss the hunt." Brittany backhanded him across the chest.

"Exactly what kind of pig are you? I'll raise fifty," Brittany spoke as she continued the game. "Gary needs to take it slow. Anything too soon would be too much. You have a son, right?" Brittany looked over toward Gary.

"Ya, I do," Gary threw in the chips to match the bet.

"Well, he has to find someone for his son, just as much as him," Brittany continued her rant.

"I'm with Adam." Peter had lit a cigar and was mumbling his words through half closed lips. "Look, man, you need to settle down again, sure. But you are a young attorney. Enjoy it. Lay some fuckin' pipe."

"Men are all the same," Preston, sitting directly across from Gary, chimed in.

"You're a man." Gary pointed out rolling his eyes.

"But he is sensitive and gets it, and I thought you were too." Brittany glared at Gary.

Gary laughed. "Hey, I'm not taking either side. I'm just listening to a good argument."

"Anyways," Brittany continued, "every new person you are with is awkward. Over and over again with one night stands? That has to be infinitely awkward. I've had a man or two even months into a relationship be awkward. It takes time to develop good sex in my book."

"Brittany, I've *had* a man or two myself," Preston emphasized, "but the awkwardness has nothing to do with it. Hell, I don't care if the sex is awkward, but I want a good cuddler, and *that* is what takes time to develop."

"I'm already a fantastic cuddler, Preston," Gary said as he folded a hand and then sipped his beer. "But I would rather have something less casual for a lot of reasons. So is this what you guys sit around and do every weekend? Get drunk and talk about your peers' sex lives?"

"I'd be happy to know more people in this world are getting laid," Victoria chimed in.

Gary had felt that this topic was a little too dangerous to begin with. It would eventually get out he was with Katelyn, and his vibrant sex life was still something he wanted to keep private. He quickly tried to change the subject. "Janice, Oliver, tell us about yourselves."

"I just started at the DA's office about a month ago. Domestic violence unit," Janice answered.

"I work for Peter," Oliver answered. "Been here about two months. And I . . ."

"*Shit*, you guys should see this." Peter had apparently become bored with the subject and ventured onto his phone. He must have seen something interesting because he sprung up and turned on the TV in the corner, quickly flipping through the channels until he found a local news broadcast.

"Yes, Kelly. Patrons early this afternoon apparently discovered the business owner's body in the back of the store when his tool rental shop appeared to be open for business, but no one was in the store. The patrons became suspicious when they leaned over the counter and apparently saw a trail of blood leading into the back-room." The field anchor Lyle Cunningham was someone who had interviewed Gary on many occasions. The scene was being shot in front of a local store, which was hard to make out. Police lights were shining in the background, and crime scene tape was swinging in the wind in a cliché manner.

"Lyle, can you tell us what police are saying about the murder?" the news anchor apparently named Kelly asked.

"Police are saying that this appears to be a crime of passion. They are not releasing the full details of the murder at this point," Lyle said in a serious tone.

"What do we know about the victim, Lyle?"

"Robert Murray is a fifty-four-year-old business man that has made his home in Klamath for several years. About three months ago, Mr. Murray was arrested for sex abuse charges against family member. Since then, he has been released on bail, and his store has been run, according to patrons, mostly by his wife. Now, we don't have any further details of that crime or if there is some sort of connection."

"Sex abuse, whose case is that?" Victoria blurted out.

"Gary, isn't that your guy?" Peter shouted toward him a little louder than normal due to being fairly intoxicated.

"Ya, that's my guy, Jesus," Gary said. A hundred things were going through his mind. He was staring at the television in stunned disbelief.

"Hopefully his check cleared," Victoria joked as she took another swig of beer.

Gary hadn't heard from Robert since their last meeting, nor had he heard back from Eddie. How could Eddie have done this? Eddie has just told him this horrific story about how he had been involved in killing someone. Now it seemed that Gary was too.

Gary was very aware that the room was looking at him, and whatever expression he had on his face was probably not one of a disconnected lawyer representing a sex abuser.

"Just never had a client die on me that wasn't a natural death, it's weird." Gary had to say something to explain the stunned look.

"Shit, I've had them stabbed by angry victims, shot by angry mothers, poisoned by angry wives," Peter began.

"Who the fuck do you know that was poisoned?" Victoria questioned.

"Well, maybe not poisoned," Peter adjusted, "but I do remember one of my guys getting a pot of boiling water thrown in his face in jail and dying a couple of days later. Also, had one get shanked.

But hell, I'm sure some of those sick sons of bitches got poisoned."
Peter downed the rest of his drink in large gulp.

"Fuck, man, that's nuts. It may be little, but this town is fucked
up," Adam blurted out. "Who do you think did it?"

Not this question, any question but this. "Hell, I don't know,"
Gary started to think as he answered. "Honestly, the crime itself was
kind of lame. I really thought we could get an acquittal. This crime
really didn't seem like the one to kill someone over." Gary decided
to go straight to the facts of the crime itself. And of course *this* crime
was not one to kill over. But the crimes committed against Katelyn?
Those were worth killing over. Or were they? It was a very real conun-
drum that Gary now faced.

"Tame sex abuse, huh?" Peter answered, laughing and shak-
ing his head. "I guess you have to be one of us to understand that.
You have to have seen some fucked-up shit." He laughed heartedly.
"Janice, looks like you'll have an interesting couple of days at the
DA's office. Hell, let's get back on track, I'm losing my buzz."

Gary spent the next half hour trying to make his way out of
the game in a swift yet not-so-obvious manner. Every time he got a
decent hand, he bet big, hoping someone with a good hand would
jump in. Every time he had a great hand, he folded immediately. But
the strategy quickly backfired. With a jack and a ten, he went all-in
against Victoria's hand when she had an obvious pair of aces. But as is
the nature of Texas hold 'em, Gary made a straight on the final card,
doubling his chips. On most other occasions, his betting scared other
players out of the hand. Finally, with only Peter and Gary remain-
ing, Gary decided the best strategy to end the night swiftly and not
created a long drawn-out one-on-one match was to go all-in on an
off-suit 2 and 7. Peter's hand made short work of it, and the night
mercifully came to an end.

"You must be glad it is Friday. Should be one hell of a week
for you." Peter stumbled through the words, snorting with laughter
through the smell of cigar smoke and bourbon. The mixture smelled
like someone had lit an old dirty sock collection on fire.

"Ya, I'll probably head in this weekend and see if his family needs anything. It was good to see everyone!" Gary yelled back at everyone still putting their coats on at the door.

When Gary got to his car, he noticed that he was more intoxicated than was advisable for driving. However, the cold air seemed to sober him up on his walk, and he would make the best of it. His office was only four blocks away, and he decided that he needed answers, and he needed to know his next move. He quickly drove to his office.

When he entered the building, he turned on the lights and made for his computer. He turned it on and made a cup of coffee while he waited it to load.

He went to the local news stations webpage when the computer finally turned on and looked for the story on the murder.

He found only a short excerpt, without much more than the original news story had brought. It made Gary more anxious than before. Gary tried to think and read through the lines. A crime of passion, the news had said. Usually, this means it looked like someone emotionally attached had killed him. A family member, a victim . . . victim's parents. It also meant that the crime was particularly violent. A gunshot wound was a gunshot wound and rarely looked passionate. It usually meant that the murder weapon was some sort of blunt object or knife. Also, it would not look like the man had been beaten in a calculated manner. It wouldn't look like he had been tortured or that someone stronger than him had killed him.

The murder Eddie had committed before was with a gun. But Gary thought, perhaps Eddie killed him on accident and then staged the passionate death? None of Gary's reasoning gave him comfort. Each thought took him to a darker and darker place, running images of what must have happened to Robert through his head, mixed with images of Eddie turning on him and a needle entering Gary's arm as he was strapped down for his last breath in prison.

Gary shuttered. He had to know. He needed the truth, and it could not wait until Monday. Gary looked for Eddie's filed in the cabinet, making a mess out of the room as he tried to find it. It was on the floor next to Gary's chair, not in the cabinet in the first place.

He found Eddie's e-mail address and went into his e-mail program only to find that Eddie had e-mailed him first: "Mr. Tornow, I'd like to meet and talk about our case if possible. I know it is the weekend, but it would be very comforting to me and my family to get an update tomorrow. Thank you, Eddie."

CHAPTER 19

● ● ● ● ● ● ●

If We Confess Our Sins, He
Is Faithful and Just

"You can't honestly think that I am going to believe that, right?" Gary was practically yelling at Eddie with the rage that had built in him overnight.

Katelyn had stayed at her friend's house the night before. After leaving his office, Gary had picked up Sam from Marti and spent most of the night lying awake in bed, awaiting his 9:00 a.m. appointment with Eddie. Sam was upstairs in the spare office that wasn't in use, playing with some toys and making quite the racket while doing so.

Eddie sighed. "I only know one thing about his death. The man chose not to die a coward." Eddie's voice was almost ominous.

"So if you know he didn't die a coward, how am I supposed to believe you didn't kill him?" Gary tried to work out the holes of logic in his head.

"Luckily for both of us, I spent the last few days in Reno. I had a nephew born. I haven't been in town since Tuesday. I got back late last night and e-mailed you after I caught the late news." Eddie's explanation created a whole new set of questions.

"Did you rough him up like we talked about?" Gary suspected that Eddie may not have gotten around to it yet.

"Absolutely," Eddie said with confidence. "Beat the hell out of him six days ago on Sunday."

"Tell me," the words barely slipped out of Gary's dry mouth.

"I sat outside of his home on Sunday morning. He got in his car and drove out to the bike trail on the edge of town. Nobody else was around. I grabbed him and pulled him off into a field. The man cried and kicked like a toddler. He began the conversation as a pussy would. So I was curious as to why you would bother with him after I saw him. He was pathetic, a little girl in a man's body."

"I gather you asked him why someone would in fact bother." Garry took a drink of soda and delivered the monotone words. He couldn't believe how ignorant he was to get involved in this.

"He seemed to think someone named . . . I think it was Corey, maybe Chris . . . anyways, he thought someone else had sent me. I didn't say that they had, but I didn't say that they hadn't. I guess he must have still thought that when we were done."

Gary recalled that the name of the victim's father was Caleb. Perhaps that was who Robert thought sent him. "So how did it happen then?" Gary felt impatience building inside his chest.

"I slapped the bitch around a few times. Then he said he was sorry. So I got him on his knees and told him to confess his sins, just as I always do. Then he told me that he had hurt someone, a grandson. Then I whipped him across the face. I told him I wanted all his sins. That he was confessing to God himself, not me. And he told me about two nieces that he had made do things to him. He told me about watching kids at the park and jacking off. He told me about cheating on his wife with a young man he found on the internet. I started to understand why you wanted him to face justice."

"You said he didn't die a coward. What did you mean by that?" Gary hadn't calmed down at all because of the explanation. Things made even less sense to him now.

"I told him he had a week to confess his sins to the world, and only that would purify him. And I told him that if he didn't, I would find him again, and the world would know his sins regardless of his approval." Eddie slowed down as he looked for the words. "And he would know pain that he had never known before."

"I still don't—" Gary began but was quickly interrupted.

"The only explanation is that the man died because someone didn't like his sins. That he manned up and confessed and someone decided he must die for those sins," Eddie answered before Gary had finished the question.

Gary sighed. "Okay, how bruised up was he? Are the police going to know he was beat up just a few days before?"

"I didn't break anything. I punched him in the ribs but didn't feel a break. The bruises, outside of his face would probably look like they came from anything, a fall or something. The pistol-whip probably left a bruise, so it depends on how he died if they saw it or not."

The thought didn't comfort Gary. Murder investigations went deep into people's lives. If Robert had left the encounter a complete secret and the murder had been particularly violent, perhaps it wouldn't be an issue.

"Okay, we won't talk about this again, private or otherwise, until we absolutely need to. I think it is best that we don't see each other unless something comes up with this or your other case. I don't want us linked together as more than client and attorney. I'm sure nobody noticed you today, but still. Let's be safe about it."

Eddie nodded, shook Gary's hand, and made for the door. "One more thing, Mr. Tornow, I'm not a snitch. If this comes back on me, I won't rat you out. Except I am a father. If the beating comes back to me, you take care of my family, and your name stays out of my mouth."

Gary had thought that at some point he would face this. He didn't know what Eddie would want, but in the back of his mind, Gary knew that Eddie would have leverage over him the moment the act was complete. This was a pedestrian request compared to the things that had gone through his head.

"Done," Gary didn't hesitate to accept. He knew that he had to keep himself safe, to keep Sam safe no matter the dollar amount.

Nothing about the conversation had truly calmed Gary. Could Eddie be taken at his word? Was he lying? In a lot of ways, Eddie's story made a lot of sense. On the other hand, it created more questions. Who else could have killed Robert? Why else would someone have killed him? Eddie had reasoned someone "didn't like his sins." True, that made sense, but who would he have told that would have killed him over it? Why would he have not told Gary before he told everyone else? A lot of questions needed to be answered before Gary would be safe.

Gary knew that Katelyn had not seen the news yet. For one, he knew that she had been with her friends last night and too preoccupied to turn on the news. Second, she was not one to watch the local news. "It is too negative," she would say.

On the way home, Sam fell asleep in the back seat only seconds after they left the parking lot. When he had picked Sam up at Marti's, he had been asleep, but he must not have been asleep long when Gary had arrived.

Gary's phone began to vibrate in his pocket. He took it out of his pocket while sitting at a light and looked at it. It was Katelyn. He answered the phone.

"Hi, sweetie, what are you up to?" Gary answered, trying to sound calm. Assuming that she did not know the news, Gary almost felt as though he was guilty of hiding it from her. He had no intention of telling her over the phone, however.

"Just got out of the shower. I had a late night last night. What are you up to?" Katelyn's voice was rejuvenating. It had a calming ability that nothing else in the world had.

"Well," Gary began, "Sam is asleep in the car, and I was headed home. I wanted to talk to you. Do you want to come over?" Gary asked with some apprehension.

"Ya, of course. Something serious?" Katelyn sounded concerned.

"Yes, but nothing bad about us or anything, just something I think you need to know." Gary wasn't sure exactly how he would tell her or how she would react.

"Okay, ya," Katelyn still sounded jostled. "Well, um, I'll be over in like a half hour, okay?"

"That sounds great, I lo—will see you then," Gary almost stumbled into the L-word.

He could hear Katelyn trying not to giggle on the other side of the phone. Apparently, the slip did not get past her. Gary felt some relief in her now-calm tone. "Okay, I'll see you then."

CHAPTER 20

● ● ● ● ● ● ●

In Nomine Patris, et Filii
et Spiritus Sancti

After pulling into the driveway, Gary took Sam in his arms and laid his head on his shoulder. He grabbed the new key to the door, the old one having been changed, and opened it up. The house was in a general state of messy disarray. He laid Sam in his bed and shut the door, trying to keep as quiet as he possibly could. Then he began to clean the house as quickly as he could, trying to work out the nervous energy until Katelyn got there. Brandon was with his father this week, so it would just be her.

"Hi, sweetie." Katelyn walked in the door. There was something very comforting about her feeling comfortable enough to walk in the home without knocking. "Where is Sam at?"

"Out cold in his room." Gary kissed her on the lips and pulled her close to him.

"You seemed pretty bothered earlier about something, you okay?" Katelyn asked with concern.

"Ya, um, sit down, sweetie," Gary grabbed her hand and sat on the couch. He didn't look up at her right away.

"What's wrong?" Katelyn gave him a puzzled look as if she couldn't possibly understand why Gary was so bothered.

"Have you watched the news the last couple of days?" Gary inquired.

"Yuck, you know I haven't," Katelyn answered with rapid disgust.

The words caught in Gary's throat for a few moments. He wasn't sure how to form the words.

"What on the news could possibly have you so bothered?" Hearing it had to do with news must have calmed Katelyn considerably for some reason, perhaps thinking there was some global tragedy she was supposed to be scared of.

"Your uncle Robert Murray was murdered yesterday," the words poured out of Gary in a rush.

Katelyn looked like she had been struck dumb over the head.

"You okay?" Gary asked with concern as Katelyn looked like she was going to be sick.

"I don't . . . I don't know." Katelyn paused. "No, no, I'm not okay."

"I'm sorry." Gary reached out and moved his right hand up and down her arm. "How are you feeling about it? It has to be weird."

"I'm not sure what to think." Katelyn had not stopped staring at the point at the wall she began to fixate on after hearing the news yet. She hadn't moved at all or acknowledged Gary's touch. Wherever Katelyn was, it was not in this room.

Gary and Katelyn sat in silence for what seemed like several minutes, but it was more likely several seconds.

"How?" The only question Gary didn't really have an answer to.

"They haven't reported that. They only said that it was a crime of passion." Gary had been teetering back and forth since he found out how involved Eddie was on whether or not he would reveal more details than the news report had. Katelyn's stunned reaction sobered Gary's senses. Regardless of how Katelyn felt about Robert, Gary realized that she would not take his involvement at any level well.

"Do you think it had anything to do with the case you were working on?" Katelyn looked up at Gary for the first time. Katelyn reached her hand over and placed it on the hand Gary had on her arm. It appeared that Katelyn's shock had begun to fade, although the look in her eyes still appeared distant.

Gary pondered this for a moment. "I don't really know, but it would be a hell of a coincidence for him to be murdered over something else when he is being charged with sex abuse." Gary decided that part of the truth would be sufficient. It was the logical conclusion, with or without his inside knowledge.

"Ya know, I thought about doing it myself," Katelyn started. "When I really knew it was him, over the last few months, I thought about it. Blowing a hole in the back of his stupid head. Heck, I even thought about what you said about if we ever killed someone together."

"*Boondock Saints* style. In the name of the Father, the Son, and the Holy Ghost. You're not a killer though." Was Gary one? Did his actions that appear to set off a chain reaction ultimately leading to Robert's death make him a killer?

"I thought him being dead was what I wanted. I thought that it would make things better." Katelyn began to stare off again.

"But it wasn't?" Gary's tone was more of a solemn statement than a question.

"Well, yes and no," Katelyn hesitated for a moment, searching for words. Katelyn shook her head, with Gary's words apparently awakening her once again from her state of astonishment. "He deserved to die. He deserved whatever happened to him, but . . ." Katelyn paused again. "I'm never going to be able to ask him why. I'm never going to be able to slap him across the face and tell him how much pain he caused me. I'm never going to be able to look him in the eyes and call him the sick son of a bitch that he is. I thought him being offed would bring closure, but it feels like it opened more doors than it closed."

"I guess closure doesn't work like that. I don't really think that it is about closing a door. I think it is more about walking through the door." Gary moved a little closer to her and put his arm around her, pulling her into him.

"So what you are saying is that looking back for answers isn't going to help?"

"I don't think it will. I think that you have to come to peace in some other way," Gary kissed her on the head.

"The only peace I can think of is the kind you get from tequila." Katelyn smiled slightly with a faint chuckle for the first time during the conversation.

Gary smiled at her. "Okay then. I think that we can arrange that."

Gary sat up and held his hand out, beckoning Katelyn to take it. She did, and they made their way into the kitchen. Gary grabbed a chair from near the table and pulled it to the countertop. He climbed up on it, opened the cabinet, and pulled out a large bottle of tequila. Katelyn had already grabbed salt from the cabinet opposite of him.

"I haven't drunk this in forever, I'm not sure if it has gone bad." Gary looked at the bottle.

It was Katelyn's turn to laugh now. "Alcohol does not work like that. For someone so smart, you can be kind of dumb." She kissed him on the cheek.

"Fine, fine," Gary rolled his eyes. "So what can we mix it with?"

Katelyn had the fridge open. "I don't think you have anything that will work for mixing. I'm going to go with shots and chasing them with cola." Katelyn had grabbed the cola in one hand and the salt in the other.

"Okay, I don't have any lemons or limes." Gary had moved over to the fridge.

"Oranges might work. Fuck it. We are drinking like hillbillies anyway. Cheap tequila, wrong fruit, store-brand cola. Classy day." Katelyn finally had a full smile across her face.

On his way back to the living room, Gary opened Sam's room and peeked in to check on him. Still out cold. How worn out could he be?

Katelyn had apparently found shot glasses in a cupboard as well. As Gary had never been the biggest drinker, only reserving it for special occasions, the shot glasses had little snowmen on them.

Katelyn peered up at Gary as he rolled his eyes at the shot glasses. "'Tis the season to get sloppy." Katelyn raised a shot glass up Gary's hand.

Gary licked the salt he had placed in his hand and took the shot in one swig. It burned like acid to the pit of his stomach.

Gary looked down, and Katelyn was already setting up her second shot. "Moving kind of fast, aren't you?" Gary smiled but put salt on his hand anyways.

"No point in drinking if you aren't getting drunk." She took the second shot as she said the word *drunk*, mumbling with the burning liquid going down her.

Gary looked down at his second shot reluctantly. "Exactly how many of these are we gonna take?" Gary knew that alcohol was in fact poison but rarely had it actually tasted like poison.

Katelyn sighed. "Fine, I guess you are right." Her tone was mockingly sweet. She smiled mischievously with only the corner of her mouth, biting her lip.

"Ugh, okay. You know that when you make that face I melt. Fine, but if we are going to do this, it's going be more interesting." Gary took the salt in one hand and reached over with his head and kissed Katelyn passionately on the neck. He then placed the salt on the spot, licked it, and drained his next shot.

"Okay, I think I get the drift." Katelyn pushed Gary down swiftly onto his back. It wasn't hard. Gary was a lightweight, and the effects of two shots almost seemed immediate. She pulled up his shirt and kissed his chest, mimicking Gary's shot.

She moved her lips slowly up to his, and he grabbed the back of her head, pulling her into a passionate kiss and intertwining his body as one with hers.

"Not yet, you don't get off that easy." Katelyn stopped Gary's hand, which had moved to unbutton Katelyn's jeans. "Your turn."

Katelyn pulled her shirt over her head and took her bra off in one swift movement. Her breasts hung perky in the air until she lay next to Gary in the small spot he was not already occupying. Gary engulfed her nipples in his mouth one at a time and then moved between her breasts. He put salt directly in the middle of her chest, licked it, and downed another shot.

After five shots, and several lost layers of clothes, Katelyn moved again to his mouth. She wore only a light pink thong at this point. Gary lay on the couch in his red boxers with his erection hanging shamelessly out as Katelyn kissed him fiercely.

Then Katelyn slowed her kiss and pulled her head down and lay down on Gary with her head on his chest. Gary pulled her tightly in.

"Why is it that I spend most of my life not able to get over the past, and then you come in and that changes? You talked about doors in life earlier. The thing is, I don't think I could have walked through this door without you. I think you are my key." She looked up and locked her eyes with Gary.

"I don't know if anyone has ever said something that amazing about me. I don't know if I'm good enough to be that. I don't know if I'm the man you think I am when you say things like that." Gary never liked compliments about himself.

"You are, and no matter what you think of you, I love you." Katelyn tightened her grasp on him, and Gary felt her hold her breath after the words poured out. Gary knew better than to think it was just the alcohol talking when he saw the look in her eyes.

"You love me? Really?" The look on Katelyn's was murderous, and Gary shifted back quickly. The initial shock of Katelyn saying the *love* word wore off quickly. "I love you too. I was just too scared to say it."

"I'm not scared of anything when I'm with you." Katelyn's passion burned brightly again as she began by kissing Gary passionately and moving slowly down from his lips. Gary sat up when she reached his stomach and grabbed her again, pulling her in for a kiss. Gary felt the passion flow through him and the strength it gave him was immense.

With Katelyn straddling his lap, Gary stood from the couch, and Katelyn wrapped her legs around Gary's waist. Their arms held each other tightly as their lips glued them together. Gary slowly walked them toward his bedroom door and kicked it open. Without looking, he turned and fell backward, landing on the bed with Katelyn on top of him.

Katelyn moved her hand down to his boxers and slowly slipped them off. Gary moved his hands to her hips and pulled her thong toward her knees. Katelyn grabbed his manhood and slid it slowly into her. She moaned loudly as he entered her. She moved up and down at a methodical pace. She began to gain speed, and she bent up to pull her hair back in a bun.

Bang.

Blood sprayed onto Gary's face and flowed down his chest as Katelyn began to gasp for air.

CHAPTER 21

● ● ● ● ● ● ●

Bloodlust

"Get off my husband, you fucking whore!" The words seemed to tear across the very fabric of time as everything slowed down. Katelyn's head fell to the side of Gary's, and he heard her struggling for air. His hands had been on her hips and moved instinctively to her back when she came down, and he felt the blood spill from her, drenching them and the bed.

Then Gary saw her, standing in the doorway, holding an old hunting rifle. Staci was shaking with tears flowing down her cheeks. The gun was still aimed right at Katelyn and Gary.

"Why would you do this to me? To . . . to . . . to . . . us!" The pitch of her voice grew high as she sobbed through the words.

Gary searched for words. Disbelief ran through him. The adrenaline sobered his instincts almost instantly.

"Staci, put the gun down. Sam is in the other room. He is going to hear this. He doesn't need to see this." Gary tried to reason with Staci in the only way he thought possible. In her right mind, Staci would not want Sam to see this. The gunshot likely woke him. Gary tried to search for more words, but nothing came to him. Fury ran through Gary, but with his gun safely at the top of the closest ten feet away, he had nothing to combat Staci with other than words and wits, and with his focus on Katelyn's limp body, Gary's wits were beyond compromised.

Gary still held on to Katelyn, her limp body lay motionless across him. He was still in her as she lay there. She continued to gasp occasionally. Gary could feel her heart still working. She was bleeding at an alarming rate, and they only had minutes until she bled out. She could not die. Before meeting Katelyn, Gary was dead. She had breathed life back into him. He felt helpless not being able to return the favor.

"Sam?" Staci shook her head, and the crazed gaze that she had locked on them began to soften. Their son's name it seemed had perhaps broken whatever trance she had been in. "Yes, yes, you are right. We shouldn't fight in front of him. It's not good for him. Well, um . . ." Staci continued to point the gun at them and began to back away. "Well, I haven't seen Sammy in a while, so I think . . . I think . . . ya, I'll take him to the park for a while. When I get home, we can talk about this." Staci turned to Sam's room, directly behind her, and then turned back toward Gary. She continued to point the gun and grabbed the doorknob, pulling the door shut.

Gary's mind moved quicker than he thought was humanly possible. He didn't know if he could safely move Katelyn onto her back as she still had a heartbeat and was breathing. Gary was afraid she would choke on her own blood if he rolled her. He slid out from under her, laying her head on pillow. He ran to the closet. He wasn't quiet about it, and Staci would likely hear him, but the pistol was not far away, and by the time she made it back, he might have it in hand.

He made it to the closet and pulled out the box. He opened it and quickly loaded the gun and ran to the door, wrenching it open. But as he gazed across the room where the door now stood wide open, there was an empty bed.

No, no, not this, anything but this. Gary felt his insides melting. He felt anguish and torment at an intensity he didn't know existed. They made him want to explode. They made him want to turn the gun now in his hand onto himself to kill the pain.

Out of the corner of his eye, Gary saw Sam's blanket lying on the kitchen floor. They must have made their way through the kitchen and down out of the basement. Gary's cell phone was on the coffee table in the living room. He made for it first, grabbing it quickly and calling 911. He held the phone between his ear and shoulder and held the gun up, making his way toward the basement. Halfway into the kitchen, he heard, "911, what is your location?"

"2055 Harvey Street in Klamath. My name is Gary Tornow. My girlfriend was just shot by my . . ." Gary hesitated for a moment, looking for Staci's proper label. "Wife. My son has been kidnapped by her. She is not supposed to have contact with her."

Gary didn't have time to stay on the phone. He needed to see if they had made their way out of the house. He tossed the phone onto the countertop and sprinted toward the basement door. He took the stairs too quickly and, after about five stairs, lost his foot and slid butt-first down the rest of them, landing hard on the concrete at the bottom.

The door to the outside was directly ahead of him. The window on it was shattered from the outside in. It swung gently back and forth as if it had been wrenched back open moments ago. They were gone.

Gary began to feel tears move down his face. He made to the door and peeked outside, noticing the gate was also swinging open. He made to the spare room, clinging to pointless hope that perhaps she made her way to her old favorite room.

The room was exactly how Staci had left it when Gary last looked. The picture that had been wrapped around Staci's cell phone the night she was taken to Phoenix House was lying on the floor in the corner she always sat in.

Gary heard sirens out in the front of the house. He put the gun on the floor. He didn't need the police to be confused on what was happening. He ran up the stairs back toward Katelyn. He heard the knocking on the door as he made it to the bedroom and ran to it in order to let them in.

"Gary, you okay, what happened?" It was John Amos, the sheriff whom he had talked to in the hospital about Staci. It was a huge break as he knew the back story. The EMTs hurried past them. "Where is she?" John said, staring at the medics.

"The bedroom on the right." Gary pointed and realized his hands were shaking.

"Let's sit down." John had put his hand on Gary's shoulder in a consoling manner and guided him to the couch.

Gary worked through the events of the day. The only lie he told was about the tequila that was sitting on the coffee table. Gary told John they were celebrating their first real weekend together. Gary didn't want the police to know any connections in the triangle that formed between Robert Murray, Katelyn, and himself.

At the end of the tale, the sheriff stared at him for a few moments. "Okay, I have to radio in that Sam is missing so we can get an amber alert out. I need the license plate she normally drives."

"Ya, sure, um, I'm not sure I know it. Wait." Gary reached into his wallet on the table and pulled out the car insurance car. Although it didn't have the plate number, it did have the VIN. "Can you get it with this?"

John nodded silently.

"Okay, let's get her down the stairs. We need her on a ventilator. Her pulse is waning." The paramedics carried Katelyn's body outside on a stretcher. It was draped in a blue blanket that they had brought in. He watched as they took her outside, unable to move.

"Does she have family I can contact?" asked John.

"Ya, her phone is in here. Let me grab it for you. I'm sure it has her mom's number." Gary walked toward the bedroom. The medics had been unable to stop her bleeding completely. Drops of blood peppered the carpet. As Gary looked down, he realized that it was just as likely the blood had come off him. He was covered in it, still wearing no clothes. He had talked to John for over five minutes without realizing that he remained completely nude. The bed was covered in blood. Little pools of it were so thick that the sheets and mattresses were not absorbing.

The sight took Gary into another emotional whirlwind. He could not lose her. She meant everything to him even though they hadn't been together very long. John seemed to know it would be hard to see the carnage in the room. He had followed Gary in and took the cell phone when Gary pointed at it.

"I better get to the hospital," Gary said out loud but thinking it more than directing it at John.

"Get showered first. You're still a mess," John told him. "So the gun you have is downstairs? Are you sure they went out that way?"

"Ya, ya, I'm sure. It's busted open," Gary confirmed.

John put his hand consolingly on Gary's shoulder and made for the door. Gary was still in shock. Still panicked. He could not lose Katelyn, but he knew now that based on what the medics had said when they the room, Katelyn was hovering somewhere between life and death.

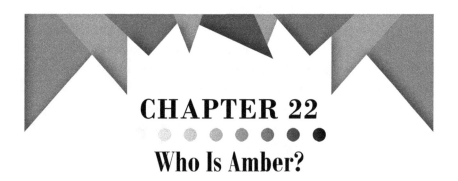

CHAPTER 22

● ● ● ● ● ● ●

Who Is Amber?

The noise coming from Gary's pocket startled him momentarily. His elbows were touching his knees as he buried his face in his hands. He grabbed the phone and read the message that accompanied the robotic shriek read:

> AMBER ALERT:
> Klamath Falls, or Amber Alert
> Update: LIC/WXL 678 (or) 2003
> Blue, Ford Taurus

The numbness he had felt did not waver. An amber alert for his own child. Never could he imagine that the madness inside Staci would turn to this. Never had he imagined that one day he would be helpless with his son in danger. He tried to tell himself that Sam wasn't in danger. That there was no way that she would hurt Sam. But then again, there was a time when he did not believe Staci was capable of harming anyone. In the last months, he had been her victim, watched her try to hurt herself, and watched her try to kill Katelyn.

Whether she was successful in her murderous attempt or not was not yet known. The ER was now full of the screeches from phones going off in unison.

"Why is it called an amber alert anyway?" Gary heard a congested woman behind him. "Who is Amber? Is it named after a girl that was kidnapped or something?"

The old woman that had apparently asked the question received an unresponsive grunt from her husband, who continued to read his newspaper. It sounded like the wife had to reach into the husband's pocket in order to clear the alert from his phone.

Gary had not been allowed in the back, not being a family member. John had given him the courtesy of letting him know that Katelyn was in surgery. John had come by to wait for Katelyn's mother whom he was only able to leave a voice mail for.

"Where is my daughter? Is she here?" Gary looked up and saw Katelyn's mother, Jerry, walk in, barking at the triage nurse. The triage nurse was frantically looking through paperwork.

John had appeared from the back and began talking to Jerry. John was trying to calm Jerry down, and he wasn't speaking loud enough for Gary to make anything out. Then very suddenly, Jerry's eyes met Gary's. John was still talking to Jerry, but she was now marching away toward Gary.

Gary stood up and tried to form words, but none came. *Wham!* Jerry had slapped Gary across the face with more force than he had imagined she could produce.

"You sick son of a bitch. This is your goddamn fault!" She was right, of course. "You dragged her into whatever bullshit was going on in your life. Your own client. Lawyers really don't have souls, do they? Did you ever think about what could happen to her? Did you even care? You took advantage of her, and she could *die* from this. Aren't there rules against dating clients?"

"We didn't date until after the case was over." This was mostly true. It occurred to Gary that Katelyn may not have told her mom that they were involved, which complicated this conversation. "I love your daughter, and I can't lose her. And she loves me."

"Love? Is that what you call this? She all of a sudden doesn't have time for her family and won't tell us why, abandons her fiancé without an explanation, and has an affair with a married man who happens to be her attorney? That's not love, it's a fucking soap opera plot. If she dies, her blood is on your hands," She had formed a finger and poked Gary hard in the chest with these last words.

"I know it seems crazy, but it isn't what it looks like. She means the world to me." Gary felt ashamed of himself beyond measure.

"I hope that her meaning the world to you is consolation enough for her son if he ends up not having a mother because you can't keep your fucking dick in your pants." Gary didn't know how to respond to the judgmental gaze Jerry set upon him.

He sat down and buried his face again. "My son has been kidnapped, and I don't have a clue where he could be. And I know that Katelyn and I have both made mistakes in handling this situation. And you have every right to be furious with me, want me in there instead of her, want to beat me. But the only two people in this world who matter to me are in peril right now. And whether or not you believe, I love Katelyn, I do. And . . . and I never, *never*, wanted anything to happen to her."

"For your sake, you better fucking hope my daughter walks out of her." John had decided it was time to intervene and had put his hand on Jerry's right shoulder. Jerry shook it off and went for the door to the back, where the triage nurse had already pushed the button for the door to open.

"Well, that went better than I expected," John said sarcastically as he sat next to Gary.

"Have you heard anything yet?" Gary didn't have the patience for sarcasm. His son was kidnapped, his soul mate was facing death, and based on the conversation he just had, his career appeared to be over.

"No," John's tone was stiff. "Since you guys are from Portland, we have been watching all the roadways up toward it. She isn't at her apartment, and nothing there gave us any kind of clue as to where she could have taken him. Is there anywhere you can think of? Anything special to her or maybe special to the both of you?"

"No, not really. We got married in a small church. We never really went on vacation anywhere expect the beach. We always talked about going to the redwood forest but never really got around to it. I proposed to her in the Columbia Gorge, but it was more a special place from my childhood than anything we shared together."

"Well, I don't think you are going to get into the back anytime soon." John checked his watch. "Look, it's getting late. Why don't you go home and get some rest? Try to figure out where they may be in town. We have the roads going out of town to Medford, Bend, Weed, Reno, and Lakeview all covered. They have to be somewhere in town."

Gary knew that the look on his face must have been one of either horror or disgust as John quickly continued.

"I know you can't rest, it's just something we are supposed to say. I know I'm not supposed to tell you anything about what happens with Katelyn, but I promise I'll update you if there is anything that changes at least with her condition." He patted Gary on the back and made for the doors to the back.

There was nothing Gary could do in the waiting room, he knew that. He was overwhelmed by hopelessness but knew he could not sit and wait for nothing to happen. He at least had to try to find where Staci had gone. He needed his son. He needed his little buddy in life.

The drive home was nerve-racking. Gary checked his phone about every fifteen seconds, looking to see if there was a call updating him on Katelyn or Sam. He also eyed every single car that drove past him, looking both for the car that Staci had left in and seeing if she had perhaps changed cars with someone. It was getting dark though, and he could not make out the shapes in the cars. Twice he swore he saw Sam sitting in a car seat in the lane next to him, and excitement grabbed a hold of him, only for him to realize that not only was it not Sam, but the kids looked nothing like him.

When Gary walked into the house, he again saw the carnage of the morning. The carpet was stained with drops of blood leading from the bedroom to the couch in the living room and out toward the kitchen. What could he possibly find that would tell him where Staci would have gone?

Nothing upstairs would give him a clue. He went back to the basement. Nothing. There was nothing down here that gave him any clue that Staci had any connection to this world expect for smoking pot. He sat on the ground and picked up the gun he had left there this morning.

He stretched out his legs and leaned his back up against the wall. Tears began to form in his eyes as the gravity of the situation weighed him down. Nowhere to look. Nowhere to run. The gun sat in his hand as if beckoning him.

Was there any place special to him and Staci? Was there any place she would take him? No, this room encompassed the entirety of what he knew of Staci, the shell of the person he married. It was true that he should have never married her in the first place, but her deterioration was steep, and this place was the only lasting monument to her. Kidnapping Sam and attempting to kill, if having not killed Katelyn, left Staci likely to be cornered and to try something desperate. Her deterioration would end in prison, but when, and how many would suffer?

Most people did not know the statistics of kidnapping, and Gary's knowledge did not comfort him. In fact, it did exactly the opposite. It had been hours since Staci had taken Sam, and every second that ticked by was precious. With her mental condition, it was unlikely that they would find either of them alive or Sam would be found alone if found at all, unless found tonight.

And Katelyn? She was shot in the back on her right side. Gary wasn't told anything by the medics, the doctors, or even John, but had common sense to know that Katelyn's lung has been punctured and lost a lot of blood. He knew that her chances of survival were thin.

His career had also gone up in flames in this one swift move of vengeance from Staci. Jerry would turn him into the bar for being with Katelyn. They had not had a chance to straighten the story out beforehand. If Katelyn survived, he would talk to her, but with her road to recovery, it was unlikely her mother would allow her to talk. If she died, the bar would care about the situation he put her in and realize that a story about them not having an inappropriate relationship would be bullshit before it left his lips.

Again, the gun in Gary's hand seemed to call to him. To remind him of the hopelessness. To remind him of the fact that his actions and his actions alone lead to the chaos of the day.

Slowly, Gary raised the gun in his arm and pointed it toward right side, in the same spot that that shot had pierced Katelyn. It was what he deserved. To feel her pain, to feel her suffering. His fault, all of it. He knew he took advantage of Katelyn. He knew that she was innocent in all of this. Her mother seemed to place blame on the way Katelyn had handled the situation. But none of it would have been necessary if Gary didn't have to keep things a secret. If they hadn't had to, perhaps they would have been away from the home when Staci came. If they hadn't had to be secretive, perhaps Staci would have already known and not had the reaction that caused her to shoot Katelyn without uttering a single word or warning.

He moved the gun from his right side to his left side, pointing at his heart. He had felt Katelyn's heartbeat every time that blood had gushed from her while she lay helplessly on top of him. Every time she gasped for air, the heart seemed to struggle more and more.

Was there anything left for him in this world? He looked around the room. He despised everything in the room, as empty as it was. It all symbolized the fall into darkness that Staci's madness had took her down. The only thing that didn't remind him of her was the picture of the forest that was left on the ground. A forest he still didn't recognize. It drove him mad that a generic picture of a generic forest could be a clue to where his son could be, and the picture was so unhelpful that it brought even more helplessness upon Gary.

Gary moved the gun from his heart toward the right side of his head and placed the barrel on his temple. Why not? Sam was lost. Katelyn would be dead by the morning. The meaning of life had been sucked away in one swoop.

Bang!

The sound rang through the whole house. But the gun still rested upon Gary's head and had not yet been fired. The sound came from the living room. A million thoughts raced through his head. He quickly stood up, with the gun still in his hand and ran toward the stairs. Thinking better of it, he stopped once he reached the stairs and slowly walked up them, trying not to make a sound.

Staci had said that she would be back later, something Gary had completely ignored as a real possibility. Was she crazy enough to actually come back to the house? Gary wasn't even sure if he had told John that she said it. When he reached the top of the stairs, he had no choice but to allow the door to screech as it opened just as it always did. He quickly looked around the corner to the kitchen. Nothing was out of the ordinary.

Gary continued to walk slowly with the gun raised and came to the hallway and saw one of Sam's shirts on the floor in his doorway that wasn't there before. He turned to the living room, and the front door was swaying back and forth. With all the thoughts going through his head, he had neglected to lock the front door and perhaps forgot to shut it. He checked his bedroom. No one was there. He quickly checked Sam's room and found the source of the loud bang. It was Sam's dresser lying on the ground. Clothes were flung all over the floor.

Gary lifted the dresser back into its normal position. It must have fallen over. Yes, that was what happened. He had left the front door open and maybe the dresser had a leg that had been loose and fallen over. Then Gary looked a little closer at the dresser. Three of the four drawers were completely empty. There were only enough clothes on the floor to fill maybe one of the drawers. And looking at the dresser itself, the legs were still sturdy. Gary did not see Staci leave with Sam, but it would have been unlikely that she could have carried Sam, the rifle, and the clothes when she left the first time.

Gary sprinted to the front door. It was his only chance, his last ray of hope that he clung to. He ran through the opened door, onto the porch, and saw a car turning the corner toward the main street. He ran back into the house and grabbed his keys and phone off the coffee table.

He didn't have any shoes on but still ran toward his car, jumping down the stairs off the front porch. He wrenched open the car door, put the keys in, started the car, pulled out the driveway, and drove like mad toward the main road.

Which way? Which way would she go? He only had a split second to decide, and he turned to the left, accelerating the car to well over fifty in seconds. In his split-second decision, he realized that turning to the right would lead out of town toward Bend in a few blocks and likely was being watched.

He continued to speed up, looking frantically for any sign of her car. Then he saw it. The road came to a T just ahead, and he got a clear view of the color of the car ahead of him as it turned, a blue Taurus.

He slowed down slightly, keeping his distance now that he realized she was in front of him. He picked up his phone in his right hand and then put it down. No, not yet. He wanted them to stop. He knew too well the tactics that police used in these situations. He knew that they would be careful with Sam in the car, but Staci was an incredibly nervous driver and not that skilled as she barely ever drove. It was highly likely that any sort of police chase ended with her wrecking the car.

He followed her for about another mile, and then she turned to the right, conveniently using her blinker. She didn't know she was being followed. The road curved around again, and Gary realized that they were now heading toward the lake.

This road also led to Medford, and Gary realized that if Staci continued on this path, his hope that this wouldn't end in a police chase would soon come to a conclusion. The streets here had no lights, and the road curving around the lake turned up into the forest.

Gary tried to maintain vision of the car, but as she turned up the highway and toward the woods, he could not see the car. Gary sped up and quickly turned the corner up the hill and into the forest. He caught a glimpse of her brake lights as she made it to the top of the hill, and then they vanished again.

Gary made it up the hill and then . . . nothing. There were no signs of her lights anywhere. How? How was it possible? The stretch of highway in front of him did not appear to have anywhere to pull off, and he didn't see any cars on the shoulder.

Then it dawned on him. He stopped immediately and turned around. Brake lights, not tail lights. He saw her brake lights at the top of the hill. He sped back to the spot about one hundred yards away and shined his lights on the area. At the very peak of the hill on the left he saw a small fence that led away from the highway. There was no road but a stretch of grass that appeared like it was used for access from time to time. He pulled the car over and got out. The grass appeared to have fresh tire tracks down it.

He got back into the car and put the gun on his lap and turned onto the stretch. It then dawned on him that he had no idea how far down she had gone and that if he suddenly appeared it may startle her and she might do something desperate. He reversed the car and parked it on the shoulder. He took the gun and his cell phone. He opened the trunk of the car and grabbed a sweatshirt that he left in there for emergencies and began to walk down the makeshift drive-way on foot. He checked his cell phone for battery life and put it on silent so that he could not get an unexpected phone call and raise an alarm.

It did not take him long to find where Staci had driven to. After walking about five hundred feet, he saw a faint glow on his right. There was still no sign of her car, but it didn't matter. Wherever that glow was, it was likely that she was there. He turned off the driveway and began walking into the woods.

The forest was thick. He kept getting scraped by branches that he could not see in the dim moonlight that was getting fainter and fainter. He stumbled once or twice, stepping into holes. The second hole felt like it almost broke his ankle. He leaned up against a large tree for a few moments before he continued. As he rubbed his ankle, he was reminded of the fact that he was barefooted. He felt blood from small cuts up and down them.

After about fifteen minutes, the forest began to clear. The faint glow he saw was a large barrel that had a fire going in it. Behind the barrel, there was a small shelter that looked like it had once been a tool shed of sorts. But the state of it, it looked like it had been aban-doned for years. Parts of the sheet metal had fallen off and been put back on by someone without carpentry skills. The ramshackle hut sat alone in the light without anyone to be seen. Then he looked to the left and saw in the dim moonlight Staci's car parked where the driveway ended. He had no way of getting to Sam safely without Staci being alerted and putting Sam in further danger.

He looked down at his cell phone. He didn't want to corner her and make her do something desperate, but he had very little choice. Doing this alone was likely to cause more problems than it would fix. He looked at the phone, and by a miracle, it had service. He called 911 and lowered the volume and began to whisper when the operator came on.

CHAPTER 23

● ● ● ● ● ● ●

Sticks and Stone May Break My Bones, but It Is Words That Really Hurt Me

Gary had made his way back through the woods at a quicker pace than he had come in at. As he exited the woods, he began to see the police lights from a distance, likely shimmering off the vast lake. He popped the trunk of the car quickly and hid the gun with the spare tire. No one needed to know he had brought it.

Three sheriff's cars and a large armored van pulled up to the side of the road.

"Gary, what the hell were you thinking coming out here by yourself?" It was John. Apparently, as the lead officer on the case, he was seeing through every facet of it.

"You told me to think about things, look for clues, I did." Gary was too exhausted both emotionally and physical to defend his actions properly but knew he had little choice. "I didn't know it was her' it was a whim. It looked like she came back to the house, and I saw a car leaving down the street; it could have been anyone. I didn't want to waste the resources until I knew for sure." A partial truth. He didn't want the cops being cowboys and getting Sam hurt. But Gary's weapon of choice was words, and they wouldn't be enough here.

"Okay, fine." John looked out into the woods. "How far back?"

"Maybe five hundred feet or so," Gary answered. "I had gone through the woods, so it took a little while."

"Okay, stay here." John went to get back into his car and the other officers who had gotten out made for their doors as well.

"What? Wait here? No way in hell." Gary needed to see this unfold, to see that every step was taken to make sure Sam was safe.

"You're an attorney, not a sheriff. That's why you called us. Let us do our job." John turned without another word.

"Wait, how is Katelyn? Were you at the hospital?" John had already got in his car and did not answer Gary.

Gary watched the van turn down the unmarked driveway first, followed by the three cars. None of their lights were on, including headlights. He watched them crawl slowly up the driveway by way of the dim moonlight.

Gary opened the car door and sat for the first time in what felt like years to his feet, with his legs hanging out of the open car door and rested his head on his left hand held up by his elbow resting on his knee.

Gary continued to sit for a few moments and waited to see if he could hear anything. After a minute of silence, Gary got out of the car and sat on the hood for a better view. He could still see a faint light in the distance. The anxiety pulsating through his veins was extreme. He didn't know what was going to happen. Miraculously though, the hopelessness that had filled him for most of the day was at bay. The ray of light that was the possibility that his son may be safe made everything manageable.

All of a sudden, he saw the forest light with blue in red lights. The purple combination was blinding. Apparently, they had made their move on the hut. Sweat began to form all over Gary's body. He was paralyzed with anticipation.

Please let him be okay. *Please let him be* okay, was all he could think as he closed his eyes.

Suddenly one of the sheriff's cars was barreling down the makeshift driveway at a higher than advisable speed and came to a screeching halt right in front of Gary.

"Gary, I think we might need your help. She needs to be talked down, and she keeps . . . Just get in the car." John jumped back in.

Gary didn't hesitate and got in the passenger seat.

"Are you going to tell me what the hell is going on?" Panic was taking over Gary's entire thought process.

"She is yelling from inside the shed, saying she doesn't have to do shit. That her husband is an attorney and he will tell us to fuck off. We can't see her or your kid. But we keep getting glimpse of the rifle barrel." John stopped abruptly.

All Gary saw when they pulled up was the barrel still with a fire going and the door of the feeble shack slightly opened.

"Our hostage negotiator is over here. His name is Aaron," Gary and John got out of the car and walked about twenty feet to where Aaron was standing behind a police car with a megaphone.

"Any updates?" John knelt down by Aaron.

"No, same shit. Is this the husband?" Aaron eyeballed Gary.

"Yes, I guess so." A technicality that Gary loathed and now felt ashamed of. "What do you need me to do?"

"We can't get her out of there. We can't get her to even say your son is in there or safe. We can't go in guns ablazin' in case the kid is in there. We are at bit of a standstill. That structure has no windows or big holes. We are completely blind."

"The last time I spoke to her, she shot my girlfriend while she was riding me. I gather that me talking to her could upset her more than help." Gary really thought that. Exactly how could he calm Staci down after the events of the day?

"She seems to still think of you as her husband and still thinks you can and are willing to help her. You need your son to be safe, use it." Aaron thrust the megaphone into Gary's arms.

He looked at it for a moment. Then slowly he raised it toward his mouth. "Staci?" His voice rang out loudly into the woods. He had shouted, yet he had needed only to speak normally for the megaphone to be effective.

"Gary? You came?" Staci was still in the shack, but he made out her words clearly as she yelled them into the silent night.

"Yes, I need you to come out. I need you to send Sam out." Gary didn't know what he could say to calm her, what he could say to save Sam.

"Why? You have your fucking whore. You don't need me anymore. You don't want us anymore. You left me in that horrible place, and I'm not fucking crazy. I don't know why you would do this, I don't . . ." Gary heard Staci's words turn to deep sobs.

"Staci, buttercup, I love you, and all I have done is because I love you. I thought you needed help, and maybe I was wrong. I want you still. I want us to grow back together." The words fell out of Gary rapidly.

"And the whore? She was fucking you. I saw that cunt fucking you. In our own bed. We conceived our son on that bed, and you tainted it with that skank." Staci's words were still mingled with sobs.

"I fucked her, yes, and I was wrong. But I love you. And I know it was wrong. I was weak. It will never happen again. Come home. I want you to come home."

"I want to come home too." Staci's sobs began to subside.

"Okay, buttercup," Gary said the words softly, and they hung in the air for a moment. "But first I need you to let Sam come see me. Is he with you?"

"He is sleeping." Staci's words were now in a clear voice. "I can bring him out."

"Lower your guns. Don't make her panic," Gary had lowered the megaphone and told John. John made a gesture to SWAT team and other sheriffs who had their guns drawn. Gary slowly walked out from the back of the sheriff car. He didn't want to be too sudden. "Staci." Gary had raised the megaphone out again.

"I'm coming out now." Staci appeared suddenly in the doorway only with Sam. She was not holding the rifle, and it did not appear that she had any other weapons. Sam's head drooped over her shoulder as she slowly walked toward Gary. Gary walked toward her as well. He tried to move slowly.

Staci had tears formed in her eyes as she moved toward Gary. She stopped about two feet away from him, and Gary stopped in turn as to not scare her off.

"I thought you had abandoned us, I thought we were over." The tears and sobs were accompanied by a smile that covered her face.

"Never." Gary looked warmly into her eyes. "How is Sam?"

"He is tired, but we had a long day today." Staci kissed Sam on the cheek, and Gary almost fainted with relief as Sam showed the first sign of life as he snored loudly.

"What is this place? Why did you come out here?"

"This is that place I kept telling you we should buy. I told you the little ranch by the lake. No one comes out here."

Gary didn't have a clue what she was talking about. "Oh, okay."

Staci readjusted Sam.

"Here, let me hold him." Gary moved forward, and Staci handed Sam over to him. Sam stirred briefly and fell quietly onto Gary's shoulder.

"He is such a perfect boy." Staci rubbed Sam's back.

"Yes, he is," Gary said. "I have to go put him in the car, I'll be back." Gary walked backward a few steps and then turned away, walking back to the sheriff's car he had come in. Gary did not look back at Staci as he approached the car. He opened the front passenger side door and set Sam gently into the seat. Sam curled instinctively into a ball on the seat and continued to snore on.

Gary looked back. Two of the officers had approached Staci. As Staci appeared unarmed, none of the officers had raised their guns again.

"Put your hands behind your back," said one of the older officers that had been on the scene. "These handcuffs are too large. Jim, come over here and hold her hands. Terry, go get the small cuffs from the van." One of the officers came over and grabbed her hands and held them gently behind her back as the other one spoke again. "Ms. Tornow, you are under arrest for kidnapping in the first degree, attempted murder, trespassing, and resisting arrest. You have the right to remain silent. Anything you say can will be used against you in a court of law. You have the right to an attorney. If you cannot afford an attorney, one will be appointed for you. Do you understand these rights?"

"My husband will be my attorney. Gary, where are you?" Staci began looking back toward the crowd, searching for Gary.

Gary shook his head. "Enjoy your time in prison, Staci Hibbard."

"Nooo. Nooo. You lied to me, you son of a bitch. Why did you do this to me? Why?" Staci began to sob violently again. The officer holdings her hands in place had to lift her up by her arms as she began to violently kick forward at another officer. "Let me fucking go. I'll fucking kill you. You stole my son. I want my son. Give me my son. Let me fucking go."

One of her hands had slipped out of the officers, and the officer immediately threw Staci onto the ground. The one that had read the Miranda rights to her jumped on her legs. A third officer came over and grabbed her hand that had come loose. Apparently, that one had grabbed the right handcuffs during the scuffle and pulled Staci's hands together, finally locking them up.

"Nooooo, you and that fucking whore. That fucking cunt deserves to burn in fucking hell. You deserve to burn in hell, Gary. Look at me, look at what you have done to me. Look at what is happening to me. You said you loved me. You said it. You liar, you fucking liar." The officers had carried her toward the car parked next to the one that Gary had laid Sam in. She spat at him, and it landed on his legs.

"Yes, I lied. No, I don't love you. No, I haven't loved you for a while. I have to go check on my girlfriend, not my whore. And as for what I've done to you and what is happening to you . . ." Gary searched for the words for a moment. "Frankly my dear . . . fuck you."

Staci continued to violently struggle but could no longer form words. She began to shake and sob violently in the officers arms. They opened the door and threw her in the back.

Gary opened the passenger door and lifted Sam up and held him close to him. As close to him as he could. He had his son. He had his son, and he was never going to let go again.

CHAPTER 24

• • • • • • ●

Knock, Knock

Sam lay next to Gary snoring. The movie that Sam had picked out for them to rent and watch that night had begun to repeat itself for the third or fourth time. Sam fell asleep peacefully while lying on Gary's chest roughly thirty minutes into the movie the first time it played. Sleep once again was alluding Gary's capture. He looked over at the alarm clock sitting on the nightstand next to him and realized that it was already six in the morning.

He could have blamed his lack of sleep on the hard-as-concrete hotel bed or the fact Sam rolled and kicked in his sleep every few minutes. But he could not explain why every noise he heard practically made him jump through the roof. The events of the last twenty-four hours had taken a great toll on Gary.

He decided to write it off as a bad job and got out of bed and made for the shower. He turned it on as hot as it could get and sat down in the tub, letting the water run through him.

Katelyn, it transpired, had made it out of surgery. However, John would not tell him any more than that. Gary had considered returning to the hospital. However, he did not think that it was a place that Sam should go. He did not want him to see Katelyn in this state. Additionally, Gary was certain that Katelyn's mother, Jerry, would still be highly unpleasant.

He also knew that he could not return home. His mattress was ruined. The carpets were ruined. God knows the trauma that Sam went through being wrenched out of bed by Staci the prior morning.

He would call a restoration company in the morning, have the bed and carpet removed and replaced, and maybe switch the rooms.

He decided that the best thing for them was to get a hotel room for a couple of days. But the noises from the hotel guests and the general creepiness of hotel rooms, even a fairly nice hotel room such as this one, did not help relieve Gary.

After about a half hour in the shower, Gary got out and found that Sam was awake on the end of the bed, watching the movie.

"Hi, Daddy, I missed this part." Sam had shown no signs of the encounter with his mother having a negative effect on him. It seemed that whatever had transpired, Staci had been gentle with Sam. Deep down, Gary felt like he knew she would be, even with the violence of the previous day. It seemed like Gary's ability to use logic was unlocked again, as anxious as he remained. The paralysis caused by the hopelessness had passed.

He got Sam into the bath next. After Sam was done, he got him dressed for the day. He had stopped and picked up some new clothes at the store when they rented the movie.

He wanted to get to Katelyn but didn't want to leave Sam. He thought about calling Marti to see if she could watch him and play with her granddaughter for a bit, but the thought of leaving Sam with anyone gave him a sinking feeling. In fact, Gary suspected that Sam was likely to be spending a lot of time out of daycare and playing in his office in the coming weeks. To have come so close to losing, he could not let him out of his reach.

After they got dressed, they got in the car, and Gary drove through a drive-through for breakfast. Sam had hotcakes and sausages, which normally Gary wouldn't let Sam have in the car, but today he thought better of it. It wasn't that he cared about the car, but Sam usually ended up with a lap full of syrup.

The hospital was only about a mile away, so before going in, they both finished their meals.

"Daddy, what are we doing here?" Sam asked. Gary had gotten out of the car and was now unbuckling Sam from his seat.

"Well, little buddy, we are going to see Katelyn. Is that okay?" Gary had lifted Sam out and was holding his hand as they made their way to the hospital door.

"Ya," Sam replied. "Mommy asked me who she was. I told her she was Daddy's friend."

"Did your mommy ask you anything else?" Gary had not breached the subject yet.

"She asked me if I got any new toys. We went camping, and she asked if I wanted to make s'mores. I didn't like 'em, they were sticky," Sam answered in a very calm voice. Gary again felt a wave of relief. Somehow, miraculously, beyond any measurable possibility, Sam made it out of the chaos of the proceeding day without being scarred. But then . . .

"When can I see Mommy again?" The question literally stopped Gary in his tracks. They had just reached the door to the hospital, and the door opened on its own accord.

"Sam"—Gary got onto one of his knees and held Sam's right shoulder in his hand—"I don't know when you are going to see Mommy again. But it may be a long time. I know she loves you and misses you, but you can't see her for a while."

"Why?" Sam was looking at the ground. He was not crying, but Gary could tell he was upset.

Gary gently brushed his hand under Sam's chin, lifting it up. "It is hard to explain, and maybe one day you will be old enough to understand. But for now, you just need to know that you will see her as soon as she is able to see you, okay?" Gary had not really expected this conversation but in retrospect should have. Staci was still his mom. And regardless of how terrible of a job Gary thought she had done, Sam would still have to bear the burden of not having his mother around when he grew up. Gary could not imagine that pain. He didn't know how to comfort his son because he understood the magnitude of the loss even in these circumstances.

"Okay, can we go camping again?" Sam had begun to look slightly more cheerful.

"Yes, buddy, someday, okay?" Gary was relieved to know that at least on a temporary basis, Sam could accept that there would be some issue of when he could next see his mom.

They made their way through the doors and to the help desk.

"Excuse me? I am looking for the room for Katelyn Gail, can you tell me—" Gary started.

"411," the help desk staff member interrupted Gary, looked up from their book briefly, and then began again immediately after answering.

Gary's palms were beginning to get sweaty. He didn't know what kind of reaction to expect from anyone. They made their way to the gift shop. Gary picked out some flowers, and Sam picked out a balloon, although Gary wasn't sure if Sam understood the balloon was to go to Katelyn or not by the time they left the store.

They made for the elevator and started toward the fourth floor. When he got off, he looked up to see where 411 was. He turned to the left. Sam was holding his balloon in one hand and Gary's hand in the other.

When he got to the door, it was open. He peeked in the room. There was no sign of Jerry. He couldn't see Katelyn yet though as her sisters were sitting on the near side of her bed.

Gary wasn't quite sure what the protocol was in this situation. He knocked on the already opened door gently.

"What the fuck are you doing here?" Caroline had stood up.

"Leave him alone. Mom isn't here and needs to mind her own damn business. And watch your mouth. Can't you see his son is with him? Let's step out and let them have a minute." Lucy had taken Caroline's hand and was leading her out of the room.

"I'm not done with you," Caroline said in a threatening tone as she passed.

"Don't worry, she is more mad at me than you." Katelyn's beautiful smile warmed Gary's heart instantly.

Gary made his way over to the bedside and sat down with Sam. "I brought you a balloon!" Sam handed her the balloon. Apparently, he did get the concept.

"Thank you, sweetie, and flowers too, I see?" Katelyn asked as Gary held the flowers.

"Oh, ya, here." Gary put them on the hospital tray. "How are you?" He took her hand in his, not wanting to hurt her by hugging her. He wasn't sure if he would be permitted to hug her or not.

"Besides the fact that I kind of sort of took a *b-u-l-l-e-t* for my boyfriend and he hasn't kissed me yet, I'm okay," she spelled out the word so Sam wouldn't understand.

Gary leaned over and kissed her. It almost brought him to tears. He spent the last twenty-four hours believing he might never get to kiss her again. That he had lost his shot at true love.

"I thought I lost you." Gary grabbed her hand again.

"I thought you had too. How is Sam?" she asked him.

"Good, when he isn't here, I'll tell you about—" Gary began.

Katelyn cut him off. "I already know. The sheriff told me what happened this morning. I didn't really fully wake up until this morning. He came by to talk to me. Also, it has been on the news." Katelyn gestured toward the television. She winced as she raised her hand.

"I'm sorry. I can't begin to explain how sorry I—" but she cut him off again.

"You don't need to be. I never really lived before you. I wouldn't trade this for anything. I love you, Gary." She smiled at him. It looked like every gesture caused her a great deal of pain.

"I love you too, Katelyn. How long do you have to be in here?" Gary wanted to take her somewhere special, somewhere she had never been. A place they could remember forever as they started their lives together.

"A few days, I think," she responded.

"How is your mom doing? Is she going to kill me when she gets here?" Gary asked jokingly but mixed with genuine concern.

"She is working today. But I don't care what she thinks. She is mad at me too. Sam, come give me a hug." She put her arms out, which he could tell caused her great pain.

"Careful, Sam!" He had ran toward her and quickly slowed down. She held him in her arms for a few minutes.

"You lovebirds had enough time alone. Sorry, Gary, but she is my sister and is kind of sort of really, really hurt, so I want to be in here with her." Lucy came back in with a smile. Caroline still had her arms crossed.

They all sat down, and for a few minutes, awkward silence set in. Katelyn then apologized to Lucy and Caroline for keeping me a secret. Caroline still did not seem impressed by the situation, but Katelyn began to tell them about Gary and hers relationship, and both Lucy and Caroline began to melt.

"That is so romantic, why doesn't a guy ever do that for me?" Caroline asked.

"It is hard for a guy to sweep you off your feet when you are always on your knees," Lucy answered.

"Jesus, you too. Can't you stop being at each other's throat when I'm on my deathbed?" Katelyn remarked.

"You are fine, just a flesh wound. Don't be overdramatic," Lucy retorted.

They talked for what seemed like ages until they heard a loud snore from Sam. He had curled up onto Katelyn's left side that didn't have the wound and fallen asleep.

"Take our little guy home, okay? I'll be fine. I love you." Katelyn kissed Gary, and he again felt the warmth roll over him.

The drive back to the hotel room was peaceful. Sam had woken up and was playing with an action figure in his car seat.

Once back at the hotel room, Gary lay down with Sam, and they began to watch another movie. Everything in life was right for once. Chaos had disappeared. For the first time in a long time, Gary looked forward to happiness, to love, to living life to its fullest. It was a strange feeling.

Katelyn had given him true love. Better than it was described by Hollywood. Better than any fairytale. It was magical beyond any myth. He didn't know what the future held for them. But he would fight for them fiercely forever. He already knew that he couldn't be without her. Knowing that he didn't have to be was the most blissful thought in the world.

What was better was having Sam to himself. Staci was gone. He knew that it would be hard on Sam, as crappy of a mother as she was, and that stung. Gary never wanted Sam to go without either of his parents, the primary reason for trying to keep his relationship with Staci going despite the struggles it had at every juncture. But this was better than any scenario that would give Sam a split home. He would have one home, Gary's home.

Sam had dozed off again in his arms while watching the movie. Gary too closed his eyes and thought to himself that absolutely nothing could ruin this. Life was as good as it could possibly be.

Gary woke abruptly what must have only been a few minutes later as it appeared the movie had not progressed far. There had been a faint knock on the door. Gary slowly moved his arm out from under Sam and made for the door.

He pulled it open. It was John and one of the deputy district attorneys, Jennifer Van Domelon.

"Hi, Gary. We need to talk for a few minutes. You got a sec?" John began.

"Yes, sure, what's up?" Gary answered.

"Look, I know you have had a hard couple of days, but this really can't wait. We need to ask you a few questions about your client that died, Robert Murray."

EPILOGUE

Three days earlier . . .

"Are you ready?" Jennifer asked the room.

No one protested. She looked over at the mirror on the wall and nodded.

"Ms. Murray, we were introduced about twenty minutes ago by your attorney James Weston. My name is Jennifer Van Domelon. I am the lead deputy district attorney in Klamath County Oregon. For the purposes of the record, this recording is a confession made by Sylvia Murray. With me in the room, along with Ms. Murray, is her attorney James Weston, Sheriff John Talpos, and Sheriff Maria Harris. Ms. Murray, we had a brief conversation before this recording began regarding your involvement in the death of your husband, Robert Murray, and the rights you have. Based on conversations with your attorney James Weston, I understand that you intend to take responsibility for his death in exchange for a plea offer that has been furnished to you." Jennifer looked up from her notes to see the reaction of the others in the room.

The women sitting across the table nodded but did not look up. She was dressed in a tan jumpsuit, and her hands were on the table, restrained by handcuffs. Her long brunette hair was knotted in several places, and she had small tears coming down her cheeks from her emerald-green eyes.

"Ms. Murray, I know this may be difficult, but I'll need you to respond audibly in order for the recording to be clear," Jennifer said in a flat voice.

"Yes, yes, we had a conversation. My attorney did with me beforehand as well," the woman spoke with a strained voice, like she had been sobbing off and on for hours.

"Okay, and I know it sounds redundant, but I'm going to go over the high points briefly with you before we continue. First, you have no obligation to talk to me. You have invoked your right to counsel and have qualified for a public defender. Mr. Weston has been appointed to you. Do you have any concerns about Mr. Weston's representation of you?"

"No," the woman said, continuing to look down.

"By pleading guilty to this crime, you will be giving up virtually all your appeal rights. Additionally, no judge is bound by the agreement you have made with us today. Although it is unlikely that it will change, it is a possibility, and therefore, I want to be aware of it. You have been arraigned for murder and pled not guilty. As a part of your plea deal, you will be required to plead guilty to manslaughter in the first degree. This deal is as follows." Jennifer peered down at the piece of paper in front of her to get it right. "You will spend seven years in the custody of the Oregon Department of corrections. You will have ten years of post-prison supervision afterward. You will pay a fine of $5,000. Due to the extraordinary circumstances that we believe led to the slaying of your husband, Robert Murray, our office found that incredible leniency was reasonable. If you plead guilty to this crime, a judge could sentence you to up to twenty years in prison. Given what I have told you, do you still want to talk to me today?"

"Yes." Again, the woman did not look up.

"Okay, as you know from our prerecording conversation, it is atypical for confessions to be recorded in this nature for most crimes. However, it is the policy of our office to both record confessions and have suspects sign transcripts of those recordings in cases involving the death of a human being." The woman nodded.

"My understanding was that we did have a judge agree to be bound by the terms of the agreement, isn't that correct?" James Weston had chimed in for the first time.

Jennifer rifled through her notes. "As yes, I have it noted here. It looks like Judge Shearer mentioned pre-arraignment that she would bind herself to any agreement that we made. However, we do not have a signature on the plea agreement. Is that going to be an issue?" Jennifer would hate all this to be for not, for Sylvia to get a chance to change her mind.

"No." James shook his head. "It is what I remember. She has never gone back on it before."

"Okay, Ms. Murray, as you know, your husband, Robert Murray, was killed at his place of business. Can you tell me what happened?" Jennifer had grabbed her pen, ready to take notes.

"You have to understand." She still stared at the table. "I don't remember some of it. It happened so fast."

"Let me start you off with the biggest part. Did you kill him?" She would need her hand held through this.

"Yes, I killed him." The woman sniffed, the tears were beginning to run down her face more rapidly.

"Okay. For the purposes of your confession, I need to know the *why* and the *how*. As I said before, due to the circumstances surrounding the murder, you have been offered leniency. I want to make a record to justify our agreement."

Sylvia Murray nodded and took a deep breath before beginning. "We went to his work together. We hadn't been talking much. I had told him that I would stand by him, that as his wife I believed him. But the truth is that I couldn't help but feel like he was guilty. So going to the store with him was a little out of the ordinary." The tears had stopped completely. A stone-face woman now stared blankly at the mirror on the wall.

"Go on." Jennifer was eager for her to get everything out.

"He had told me that he was worried. He told me that he had to show me everything in the store, how to run it. I didn't really understand why. We had been at the store for about a half hour, and I asked him about a hundred different ways why we were there. And then . . ." Sylvia paused, looking for the words. "Then he told me that he had been visited earlier that week. He said he didn't know by who, but whoever it was, they knew everything. I didn't really understand what he meant. He didn't make a lot of sense. He said that someone had been sent to make him pay for his sins. He took off his shirt. He was bruised badly around his ribs. He had come back from his run on the bike path with blood dripping out of his mouth a few days earlier. But he has said that he had fallen."

"Did he change his story?"

"Yes," Sylvia continued. "He said he was attacked. At first, he said that he thought he was being mugged. But the guy didn't want anything. He knocked him down and kicked him in the ribs. He hit Robert in the face with a gun, which I guess explains the blood. He had thought that the guy was sent by Caleb to beat him up."

"Who is Caleb?" Jennifer was rapidly writing all this down. This story got more and more bizarre.

"Caleb is my son-in-law. Robert's crime was against Caleb's son," Jennifer answered.

"Robert was facing sex abuse charges?"

Sylvia nodded only at first and then realized she hadn't said anything. "Yes, sorry. But um, Robert said that the man knew too much. That he couldn't know everything because no one had ever known everything. I pressed him, and he told me that the person, he kept calling him an angel, told him to confess his sins. Then he told me. He told me that it was true. That he had touched our grandson."

"Is that when you killed him?" Jennifer had not looked up.

Sylvia was shaking her head, and tears once again began to form amid loud sobbing. "No, no. I began to cry and asked him why he did it, how he could do it. I had spent so much time protecting him. I lost my daughter and my grandchildren because I was protecting him."

"Did he answer you?"

"No, no, he began crying too. He just stood there." A look of disgust crept across Sylvia's face as she spoke. "He told me that his lawyer had a deal for him, that he wasn't going to have to go to jail. But he told me he was afraid. Afraid that if he didn't tell everything that he would be killed. That the angel that had been sent to make him confess would destroy him if he didn't say everything. I asked him what he meant. He calmed down and hesitated for a moment. Then he told me that he had three nieces. I knew his brother was in prison. I never met him though. We have been married for about eight years. Anyways, he told me that he had . . ." Sylvia looked more and more uncomfortable. "He told me that he hurt them. He had done the same thing as he had done to our grandson. And that's when I lost it."

Sylvia had stopped talking and sat in silence.

"I need to know what happened next." Jennifer was gentle as she needed Sylvia to press on.

"It was just there. I was standing next to a workbench, and he had come close to me. I couldn't take it that he hurt all these people. I couldn't handle it, and the hammer was right there. I grabbed it and swung it, and it hit him in the face." Sylvia had returned to a blank stare.

"What end hit him?" Jennifer needed the details in order to properly wrap up the case.

"The flat end. The blunt end, I guess it is called. He fell down, and I just . . ." Sylvia's face had horror written on it as she continued. "I just kept hitting him. He tried to talk a few times, but I didn't stop. I couldn't stop. Then after about five hits, he stopped moving."

"Okay, thank you, Ms. Murray. I am satisfied with your confession and based on the circumstances, I believe the leniency we have considered for you is indeed justified. I do have a few follow-up questions for you, okay?"

"Sure." Sylvia was wiping tears from her eyes.

"Counsel, what are you going to—" Weston began.

"I just need to ask her about this angel, and I have a few follow-up questions about things that Robert had said," Jennifer cut him off. "Ms. Murray, do you think it is possible that Caleb did indeed know the person that attacked Robert?"

"I don't know. Robert didn't seem to think so. He said that he looked Mexican, someone he had never seen before."

"Do you know anyone that could possibly know about both your grandson and Robert's nieces?" Jennifer asked.

"No, I don't think so. I mean, Robert's arrest was on the news. It is possible that someone who knew about the nieces could then know about both. It might be the nieces themselves. Or maybe it is someone that somehow knows both Robert and the nieces. This is a small town."

ABOUT THE AUTHOR

George McCoy is a practicing attorney in Portland, Oregon, focusing on medical malpractice and personal injury. He has handled a variety of cases, including medical malpractice, wrongful death, sexual abuse, racketeering, and divorce. George began his career in Klamath Falls, Oregon, after the economic collapse of late 2000s. Inspired by the variety of case types he handled early in his career in rural Oregon, George uses his experiences to bring the audience closer to the real-life struggles experienced by attorneys juggling numerous clients. In small towns, cases run together, and everyone knows everyone.

A graduate of the University of Oregon School of Law in 2009 and Washington State University in 2007, George now lives in southwest Washington with his wife and four children. George hopes that his writing will inspire others to write about their unique experiences and challenges they face in their chosen career fields.